THE MT. OLYMPUS ZOO

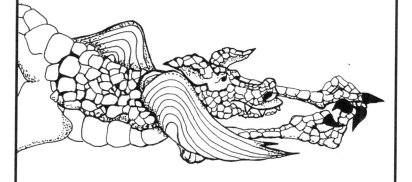

Published by
Lion Stone Books
4921 Aurora Drive
Kensington, MD 20895

Cataloging-in-Publication Data

Lowenstein, Sallie
The Mt.Olympus Zoo / Sallie Lowenstein
p. cm.
Summary: The Powers children go on a dreaded summer vacation to explore off-the-beaten-
track zoos in the Applachian Mountains only to discover a Zoo full of "real", world wide,
mythological beasts and to become involved in a series of unexpected adventures as they
tour the zoo and learn about the beasts.

ISBN 0 - 9658486 - 0 - 4
[1. World Mythology - Fiction   2. Fantasy - fiction
3. Mythical beasts - Fiction   4. Brother and Sister   5. Travel- Ficton]

Library of Congress Catalog Card Number: 97-12045

First Edition
Manufactured in the United States, July 1997

THE MT. OLYMPUS ZOO

A Novel Written and Illustrated by
Sallie Lowenstein

MYTHOLOGICAL REFERENCES
Compiled and Written by
John Kenney

Lion Stone Books

To my mother and father,
who made my childhood so wonderful

CHAPTER 1

"School's out!" my best friend screamed every year on the last day of elementary school as he raced down the hill to a summer of warm days and swimming pools, of popsicles and play.

For my sister Olivia and me, vacation was a dreaded word, for it meant we faced another of my father's notoriously eccentric, family plans. One summer we had spent our vacation crawling through tiny, black, muddy caves in the ground. Another we had spent avoiding the angry kicks and hisses of ostriches on an Ostrich Farming Adventure. This summer Dad had announced his plans already.

"Great idea this year, kids. I bought a packaged tour of odd-ball, off-the-beaten-track zoos in the Appalachian Mountains. Sounds terrific, doesn't it? Just wait, you'll love it."

That's what he always said, "Just wait, you'll love it." Olivia and I were still waiting.

"Hey, Nicky," Olivia greeted me glumly outside her classroom.

"Hey, O," I answered. "Guess we should get home and start packing."

"I guess. Nicky, do you think there's any chance this year Dad's vacation will be fun?"

"Don't count on it O."

Worst of all, Dad had taken off extra time so we could see all the zoos in the package.

"Nicky?"

"Yeah?"

"How come we have such a weird dad?"

"I don't know, O. Just be grateful Mom is normal or we could have ended up like Dad," I commiserated.

"Nick, I'm not going to marry anyone like Daddy," my seven-and-a-half year old sister said.

"Yeah, O. That's a good idea."

We got home to find Mom and Dad down on their elbows looking over maps spread across the living room floor.

"Cookies and milk in the kitchen, kids," Mom said. "How does it feel to be through with elementary school, Nick?"

"Okay," I said as Olivia escaped to the kitchen. "Mom, could I talk to you for a moment in my room?"

"Sure Sweetie," she said, following me to my room.

"Mom, why do we have to go on all these weird trips? Nobody else does. Why can't you plan our vacation for a change?"

She sighed. "Nicholas, this is the only thing your dad really looks forward to all year. How can I take that away from him?"

"I don't get it, Mom. He's got a responsible job, he's a nice guy, he dresses normally, he has normal friends, he has normal kids, he has a normal wife. What happens to him when vacation time comes? Is it like the full moon and werewolves or something?"

She just shrugged. "Why don't you get comfortable and have a snack. Maybe this will prove to be the vacation of a lifetime."

"Yeah, maybe, but more likely the vacation of the wrong lifetime," I muttered.

CHAPTER 2

"Over the mountains and through the woods, to a zoo we go, Dad knows the way, to drive the car," Olivia piped next to me in the back seat. The road didn't go over a mountain and it didn't have any spectacular views. Mainly O and I fought over who had more room and watched forest-green roll by our windows. Once in a while we saw an obviously hand-lettered sign saying: "ZOO AHEAD" or "VISIT THE FABULOUS PETTING ZOO, 2 MILES ON THE RIGHT."

"Dad," I said. "This doesn't look too good."

"Come on Nick, it's going to be great. Give it a chance, son."

"There, TURN, Harold," Mom yelled abruptly.

"Take it easy, Martha," he said, turning the car sharply.

The little road humped along while gravel spit out from under our tires, pinging the paint on our new car. The road stopped at a big sign that sang out in neon pink letters:

PETTING ZOO EXTRAVAGANZA

SAFEST PETTING ZOO IN THE WORLD

THE ZOO WHERE NO WILD ANIMAL

IS

TOO FIERCE, TOO FEROCIOUS, TOO VICIOUS, TOO VILE TO BE PETTED!

Olivia and I got out of the car reluctantly. Dad and Mom were already showing the ticket woman our passes and going through the gates.

"Anything we should, uh, know before we pet your animals?" I asked the lady who stood at the gate.

"Naw, Kid," she said through her chewing gum, working her jaw while she spoke. "Just don't feed 'em, okay?"

"Sure," I said, joining my family who were already at the first exhibit.

"How is it?" I asked.

Olivia pointed.

"You've got to be kidding? " I said, trying to choke back laughter.

We kept walking, but every exhibit was the same. The lion, the gorilla, the jaguar, the viper, were as safe as goldfish, as quiet as mice. All were made of cast concrete.

"Dad," I said, trying to keep a straight face, but smirking all the same. "This is the best joke yet."

He shot me a dirty look and nodded sadly.

"Did you see all the animals?" the lady asked as we left.

"Sure," I said.

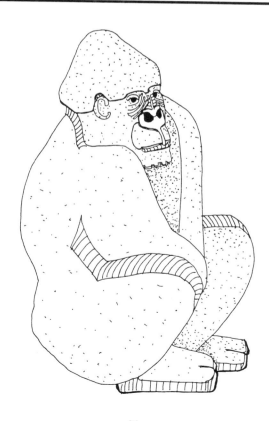

"Didn't have no problems with any of the animals, did you?"

"Naw," I told her. "None. We didn't feed them either."

"That's good, son," she answered seriously, still chomping hard on her gum.

"O," I said as we climbed into the car, "that lady with the gum is nuts."

"Sure, but oh well," she said shrugging and making a cuckoo sign at Dad behind his back.

CHAPTER 3

The next zoo on our list was a reptile zoo. It was behind a small, brown, clapboard house in the middle of a one street town. The brochure said it had two of the most unusual reptilian species around, and it did. It had a very large Komodo Dragon and a Chinese Alligator and that was all.

Dad was pretty put out because it had cost him ten dollars an adult and six a kid to see two animals and both were lethargic at that. The Komodo was a big, doughy looking thing, that moved as if it was stuck in molasses and the Chinese Alligator lay in the dirt like a log with its spiky teeth hanging over its lower jaw.

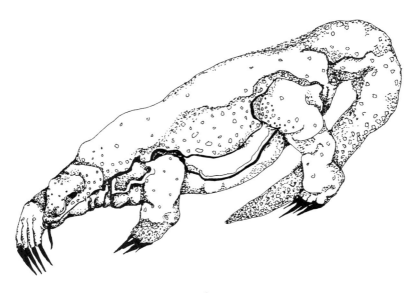

Despite Dad's muttering, I thought it had been pretty neat because I'd always wanted to see a Komodo, and most zoos didn't have Komodos or Chinese Alligators. Olivia thought the Komodo was gross, especially when she found out its saliva was deadly. Mom made us all take six steps back from the edge of the enclosure, even though the Dragon was sleeping with its head stuck in a log and only seemed to waggle its bulky, grey rear-end and tail from side to side.

"Martha," my dad said as we climbed back into the car again. "So far this is a bit disappointing, don't you think?"

"No, Dad," I said quickly. "This has been great."

I could see him in the rear-view mirror as he raised his eyebrows. "Martha, does he have a fever?"

"Well, what's next, Dad?" I asked undaunted, ignoring his comment. "I'm getting into this trip."

"I wonder if you and I will ever be in sync, Nick?" he asked.

I just smiled at Olivia as we pulled off to our next stop. I loved being contrary where Dad's

trips were concerned, but this time I was being honest.

After miles of quick turns and long stretches of one lane roads through whistle stop towns, we finally turned onto a dirt road.

"Martha, this couldn't be right," Dad said.

"But it's what the map shows," Mom answered.

"But . . . well, look Martha, are you sure we're not lost?"

"Harold, you're always sure I've gotten us lost, but I haven't this time. This is what the directions say to do."

Dad sighed and started down the road, trying to avoid ruts and pot holes. There was no sign of civilization except for an old, stone wall posted with no trespassing and no hunting signs. It seemed to go on forever.

"This is spooky," Olivia said. "Daddy, what kind of zoo is this one?"

"It's called the Mt. Olympus Zoo."

"What's that mean?"

"Mt. Olympus was the home of the Greek

Gods," I explained. "Why do they call this zoo that, Dad?"

"Got me. This is supposed to be the surprise in the tour. I'm not sure the travel agent knew. But so far, it's all been a surprise, so this must be one heck of a gag."

"Daddy," Olivia whispered. "This is weird."

"You know Olivia, I agree with you."

"Aw shucks," I smiled, "I like it. What would summer vacation be without a weird trip?"

"Can it, Nick," Dad said loudly.

The road stretched on, the trees getting bigger, the fields getting rockier, until we realized we were climbing sharply.

"This is one zoo no one comes to in the winter," Mom commented uneasily.

Without warning the road leveled out and we could see over the edge into a cloud covered valley. The road twisted around the mountain like a snake, slowly inclining upward until it dead-ended into a grassy field. Dad stopped the car.

"Well, I'll be!" he exclaimed happily. "This is actually impressive."

At the edge of the field were massive stone gates, complete with gargoyles perched atop columns. We got out and followed a path to the gates. Dad grabbed a heavy, lion-headed knocker and rammed it on brass doors decorated by twisted reliefs of animals and beasts. The sound echoed around the mountain top, finally fading away to silence. Nothing happened. Dad was about to try again when one of the gargoyles detached itself and began buzzing around our heads.

"Hi," it finally said, "my name is Gideon P. Gargoyle IV. Are you the Powers family? If so, you're late."

"Why yes, we are, but I didn't know we had specific reservations," my dad said.

"People! They are never, ever punctual. That's why Grant up there," he said pointing to another gargoyle, "claims he's sulking. He hates tardiness, but the real reason he's grumpy is that while we were waiting for you, he lost at Domination, the game of world conquest."

"Nick," Olivia whispered. "These are great special effects."

"Special effects?" Gideon hissed. "Special effects! I'm not some kind of puppet. I'm flesh and blood, little girl. Here, feel my hand."

"Yuck," Olivia said, as she delicately touched him. "You're greasy."

"Quite right. I have avoided bathing for the last, oh, five or six years."

"Phew, you smell like it, too," I said catching a whiff.

"Well, while you discuss this odoriferous phenomenon of special effects, I'll go fetch The Keeper," Gideon announced as he flew through a round hole at the top of the gate.

We waited. Nothing happened. After ten minutes, Olivia and I started staring at Grant, but he remained stonily immobile, sculpture-like.

I shook my head.

"Special effects," Olivia repeated.

"Looks that way," Dad said. "But what fun."

Ten more minutes and finally the gates creaked open with impressively heavy groaning. Gideon whizzed out and buzzed us, whizzed back and perched on the shoulder of a slightly bent, wiry old man, with a beard so long it

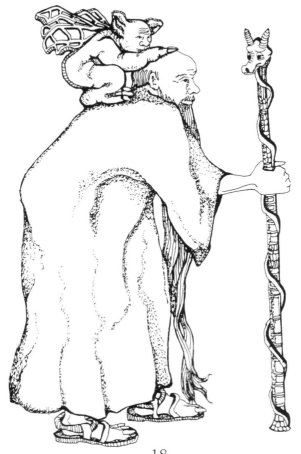

brushed the ground. He was dressed in a white, cotton shift with wide sleeves and leaned heavily on a golden staff. When he lifted his face, I was riveted by a pair of golden eyes, centered with dark brown pupils.

"Contacts?" Olivia suggested.

He reached out to shake Dad's hand. His fingers were short and stubby, but ended in inch long, blue nails.

"At least he's not a stereotype," I whispered to Olivia.

Gideon gave me a dirty look, but The Keeper ignored me all together.

"Mr. Powers," he said in a gravelly voice. "We expected you sooner. There is much to see here, and since the day is half over, perhaps we should arrange for you and your family to stay in our guest quarters overnight. No charge."

"Why yes, that would be quite nice of you," Dad said, smiling happily.

"Gideon, go arrange for it," The Keeper instructed.

"Oh brother, more work for the weary and all because humans are never on time," he complained as he sped off in a flap of wings.

"He's a bit rude, but invaluable to an old man of weak legs and great age such as myself," The Keeper said in a kind of apology. "Now then, let me show you a map of our zoo and you can decide where to begin. It's quite extensive you see," he said while he pulled a rolled-up, parchment document out of his sleeve.

"This is better than those super-dooper, movie company, amusement parks," Olivia said.

"Thank goodness," The Keeper said. "Such fakery as theirs is offensive to us."

Olivia and I exchanged glances. The Keeper sure played his part well.

"Come now," he said leading us through the gates into a large courtyard. Around its edge was a frieze depicting beasts and beasties of mythology. In the center of the courtyard was a large, polished stone with short benches set around it. It was here that The Keeper spread the map. "If you look around the courtyard, you will

notice many doorways. Each door is the entrance to a realm. Each realm is accessible only from this central courtyard, all paths beginning and ending here. Since there is such a short time before dusk, I would encourage you to undertake only one path today. Although it had been my intention to act as your guide, an impending birth demands my attention and I must ask Gideon to act in my stead."

"What?" Gideon shrieked, flapping off The Keeper's shoulder where he had come in for a return landing a few seconds before. In an extravagant display of indignation he begged, "Please, no, no. Not me. It's too much respon- sibility for a dolt like me."

The Keeper just smiled and patted Gideon's head where he hung in mid-air.

"Remember to have our guests back by dinner, Gideon," he said as he strode off, sleeves flapping.

"Darn, double darn, triple darn. I had an afternoon card game all set up. Stupid humans," he said slumping on top of the table where he had landed. "It's not fair."

"He sounds like you, Nick," Olivia said.

"Okay, let's get this over with. Pick a gate," Gideon instructed.

Olivia pointed to one with blue stones around it.

"Aquatic, hey? So be it, small human."

The path was a mosaic of tiny blue and green stones inlaid to form patterns of animals in water. The first stop was a platform on which a potted tree was growing. Its limbs dangled over a large pond, weighted down by heavy green and red fruits.

"This is a very rare species. The MBWF has put it on the threatened with extinction list."

"What's the MBWF?" Mom asked.

"The Mythical Beast Wildlife Fund, of course," Gideon answered with disdain.

"Oh," Mom said with a smile. "I see."

"I don't," Dad said. "Where's the beast?"

"This sign says its a Tree Goose, Dad," I said. "Anser arborus. Range: the coasts of Northern Europe. Gestation: Fruits ripen within eight to ten weeks. Immature when green, ripe when red. Origin: Medieval Europe," I read.

"Quit gabbing and watch those red fruits," Gideon said. "See the one half way up? We've been waiting for it to hatch for days and it looks ready right now."

At that moment it burst, sending out a wild spray of raspberry colored juice, followed by a spray of water as a small, wet gosling dropped with a plop into the pond. As it shook out its down and paddled gracefully into the middle of the pond, feathers seemed to sprout wherever water touched it.

"Neato," I said. "How'd you do that?"

"I did nothing. I promise, there is no chicanery here," Gideon said.

"How do you think they really do it, Nicky?" O asked me. "It's pretty convincing."

"Got me, but it's fun. Come on, I wonder what's next?"

We stopped at a bridge across what appeared to be a small river or large stream.

"Before we proceed to the next animal, I need to remind you to remember your manners in order to protect yourselves while visiting it," Gideon announced.

"Fine," Dad said.

"The Kappa is now extinct in Japan. It is a unique species, most like your duckbill platypus

in its combination of unlikely attributes: monkey head, tortoise shell, shallow concavity in the crown of its skull containing its life fluid. It supplements its diet with small fish and aquatic plant life. There," Gideon pointed as the Kappa surfaced and crawled onto a rock to sun itself.

When I opened my mouth to protest an obvious fraud, Gideon clamped a foul smelling wing over my lips.

"Remember, courtesy or you might regret it. Read the sign."

"Kappa. Range: rivers of Japan. Gestation: five months. Prey: discourteous humans. PLEASE DO NOT FEED THE KAPPA. BE POLITE!"

"Okay," I said, holding back my laughter, seeing that Mom and Dad were also smiling, but Olivia, who was looking through our binoculars, scratched her head.

"Nicky?" she asked as we left. "Do robots or animated animals eat real fish? Cause, I saw the Kappa swallow a fish."

"Special effects, O. Good ones, but special effects."

"If I hear those two words one more time, I'll find someone to feed you to," Gideon said, breathing foul breath into my face.

"Okay, okay. I'm sorry. I thought that was the whole point."

"Nicholas," Gideon pouted, "have you ever heard of an animated robot who could respond to whatever you said, like I do?"

"Well, yes. In lots of Sci-Fi stories."

"But," Dad admitted, "no one has actually managed it yet, Nick."

"No one we know of," I said, sticking to my theory.

Dad smiled. "Well Nick, I hope you're right for once."

"Hey," Olivia said excitedly. "What's that ship doing in that lake?"

It was actually a galleon, sails billowing at full mast.

"Who would leave a ship anchored with its sails full out?" Dad asked.

"Oh, it isn't anchored. Come on aboard," Gideon instructed, turning cart wheels in the air amidst the fluttering sails. "This fifteenth century ship is held steadfastly in position by several fish called Remora. Despite their minnow-like size, their strength is renowned. Our collection consists of only three specimens, as they are extremely hard to catch."

"Three fish hold this whole ship in place?" Mom asked skeptically.

"Now that, you can't expect us to believe," I chortled.

"As you wish, Nicholas, but the word Remora means 'ship holder' and they can be found throughout the world."

"Just not caught," I pointed out.

"Humans!" Gideon exploded. "Well, you'll be able to see the next creature clearly."

Perched on a yard arm, Gideon gave a long whistle. Before I could blink, an animal popped out of the water alongside the ship, barking loudly as it simultaneously thumped its beaver-like tail and flailed its webbed forepaws.

"Sea Dog, also know as Canus aquaticus. What few specimen are left range along the

Mediterranean Coast of Europe. He's quite friendly really. Here Nick, throw him this."

Gideon tossed me a slimy ball which I quickly flung high into the air. The Sea Dog sprang up, catching it in his mouth like any well trained dog, his body reflecting sunlight off his scales.

My father was shaking his head. Gideon flew up to him and tapped him with a finger. "Mr. Powers, do you doubt our veracity?"

"Honestly, Gideon, I don't know."

"Humans are notoriously unimaginative," Gideon sighed.

"I suppose that's true."

Gideon was leading us down the trail when Olivia called, "Wait a minute, Gideon. My ring just fell off my finger and I want to look for it."

"Oh no, not another ring. Quick, find it,"

he said, buzzing about frantically in what seemed to be an overly dramatized performance.

"For heavens sake, Gideon," Dad began. "It's only . . ."

"NO!" Gideon screamed suddenly. "Too late, too late."

"What's too late?" I asked.

"Too late," Gideon repeated. "The Ghormuha has it by now."

"Has what and what is a Ghormuha?"

"That," he said pointing at a one legged, humanoid figure topped with a horse head. "I told The Keeper they were a mistake, but did he listen? Did anyone listen? And now it'll be my fault again that someone has lost their ring."

"Somebody else lost a ring, too?" Olivia asked looking at Gideon.

"The other day this stupid lady let her kid play with her expensive, gold ring as we walked along. The kid dropped the ring and the Ghormuha scooped it up and there was nothing I could do, and that dumb woman really raised a fuss. She told The Keeper it was all my fault and threatened to sue us. And now this, and when

I'm the guide again. But, it isn't my fault. Just bad luck, bad luck. "

"I can see it wanting gold, but why would it want a dime store ring?" Mom asked.

Gideon didn't seem to hear her. He just went on lamenting loudly, "It's a pack rat. It'll take anything. Hold onto everything else you own, don't drop a thing or . . ." He stopped. "Dime store ring? You mean it wasn't valuable?"

"Nope," I said.

"You aren't going to complain?"

"No," Olivia promised solemnly. "I won't tell if you don't want me to."

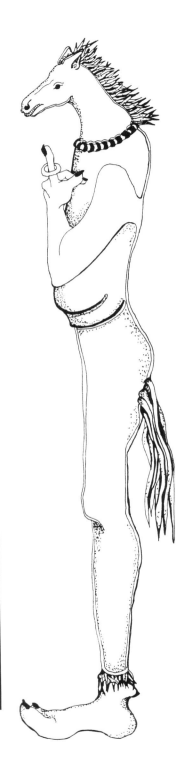

"We'll buy her a new one when we get home," Mom said, "but Gideon, if they're such a problem, why do you continue to house these things at the Zoo?"

"It's not that easy. They're next to impossible to catch and they multiply quickly. They should never have been let loose. Let's get out of here before they take something that is valuable. Come on."

"Gideon," Olivia called. "Do you have a Sea Serpent?"

"Actually, we do, although it's a young one, as our lake can hardly accommodate a full grown one."

"Can we see it?"

"Yes, but there's only time to see one more animal before dinner. Wouldn't you rather see a Sea Lion?"

"I'd rather see a Sea Serpent."

"Okay, but don't be disappointed. It's only about three years old, so it's not very big. When it's six or seven, before it gets too large to transport, but is able to take care of itself, we'll release it back into the wild."

"Where are they found?" Dad asked.

"Sorry, Mr. Powers. Humans are notorious for their destructive abilities and have been pursuing and slaughtering Sea Serpents for years. So, that's priviledged information."

"I can see your point," Dad said, winking at Olivia and me.

We followed Gideon along the edge of the lake until we came to a stone overlook. He reached into a bin and threw a few fish into the water. Something not quite definable snapped them up. Gideon flew near the edge of the water, extending a fish until something began to surface. Suddenly he shot straight up into the air, holding the fish just out of reach as an immense, glimmering head reared up and up on a long, scaly body, vaguely reminiscent of a snake. Gideon dropped the fish at the last minute into gaping jaws, lined in fine, silvery teeth. The Sea Serpent snapped back into the water like a rubber band and vanished into a frothing whirl-pool of bubbles.

"Wow!" Olivia exclaimed.

"Something, hey?" Gideon asked, obvious-ly pleased at her reaction.

"Something, okay," Dad said. "How big did you say it will get to be when it's full grown?"

"No one has ever tried to measure one."

"BIG, Dad, real BIG," I said.

"Right, if that's a baby."

"Quite right," Gideon said. "Now let's head back. Dinner will be served in about forty-five minutes and I'm starved."

"Dinner sounds like a very nice idea," Mom agreed.

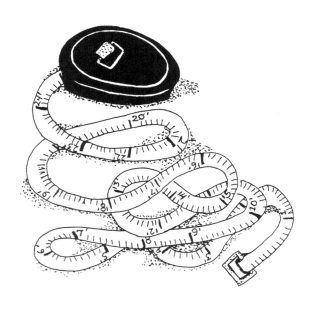

CHAPTER 4

"We rarely have guests for dinner," The Keeper said. "I hope you'll enjoy the menu. It's a bit eclectic. A little something from India, a bit from Greece or China or Turkey or Benin."

"Sounds fascinating," Mom said happily.

"Any good old, American burgers and fries?"

"I'm so sorry, but no," The Keeper said.

"Nick," Mom said in the tone of voice that meant I was being rude.

"Sorry," I said.

We had entered a room occupied solely by a large plank table, with benches on either side. The legs of the table ended in the claws of lions and birds and at each end stood a gold encrusted chair.

"Please, Mr. Powers, Mrs. Powers, do us the honor of heading the table tonight. Olivia, Nicholas, how about sitting in the middle of the benches," The Keeper indicated. "All right Gideon, call everyone."

Gideon hit a large, brass gong and immediately there was a rush of foot steps and a flurry of wings. About fifteen men and women of all ages and shapes, all dressed much like The Keeper, dashed in at the same time that five, grey Gargoyles plopped themselves down next to me on my bench. Lastly, somewhat more calmly, a tall, young woman appeared at the table.

"Let me introduce you to Dr. Lang, our veterinarian."

The woman nodded, but said nothing as she sat at the corner near Mom. I noticed one of the Gargoyles was conversing rapidly with Gideon.

"Grant, meet Nicholas Powers," Gideon said.

"Hi," I said. Boy, this got better and

better. I wondered what the Gargoyles would do with their food. To my amazement they chewed and swallowed their shares, commenting with gusto on the quality and flavor. I found I'd barely eaten I'd been so busy watching and listening to them, when my plate was whipped away and desert was set in front of me in the form of a pomegranate.

"Fruit of the dead, you know," Gideon laughed. "Eat hardy, young Nick."

Actually, I liked pomegranates and did just that, but Olivia only picked at hers.

Everyone vanished as quickly as they had come and we were finally escorted to our room. The walls were stone, hung with tapestries like some medieval castle. The ceilings were upwards of twelve feet high and a huge fireplace took up one whole wall, a window taking another. Wash basins of clean water sat on tables alongside linen towels, and goose-down coverlets adorned the feather beds.

Olivia jumped ecstatically into the fluffy mattresses and sank with a wild giggle.

"Now, to the bathrooms which are down the hall and then right to bed," Mom instructed.

"Amazing place," Dad said. "Pretty convincing, I must say."

"Well, Dr. Lang is convinced. She has been here a year helping with captive breeding, of all things. She works with the native animals that live within the boundaries of the zoo if the occasion arises, but mainly she works with the mythical animals. She showed me a scar on her wrist she got from one," Mom said.

"Martha, I doubt if she is a real vet. I'd love to know who thought this gimmick up, wouldn't you, Nick?"

"Yeah, sure, Dad. It's great. It's almost too convincing."

"Oh, come on gang. Don't go off the deep end. It's a great presentation, but whoever heard of a Tree Goose?" Dad insisted.

"Me, Harold. In a mythology class I took in college," Mom said. "This is a very well researched institution. Very well researched."

"Mom," Olivia said. "Is Gideon real? He chews and swallows food and he's funny. And, he smells real."

"Too real," I added. "Do you think The Keeper could get him to take a bath?"

"Look guys, Nick and I are going to get the luggage. We'll be back in a few minutes," Dad said, ending the conversation.

Outside it was foggy and a heavy dew covered everything. Coming back from the car, Gideon popped out next to the gate. "We're having a game of poker. Want to join us?"

We peeked around the corner and three Gargoyles and two young keepers were hunched around a crate.

"Sorry, Gideon," Dad said. "We're exhausted."

"Another time, then."

Going up the stairs, I felt more and more uneasy. Something was just too good not to be real.

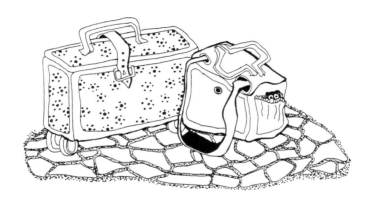

CHAPTER 5

Breakfast was delivered to our rooms at sunrise. Groggily we began to eat. The trays were laden with corn bread drenched in fresh churned butter, oatmeal doused with raisins and brown sugar, omelets filled with crab meat and vegetables and a huge bowl of berries and kiwi and mango. We were feeling stuffed and ready to be lazy when Gideon knocked on the door.

"Come on," he chattered with unbounded energy. "Hurry up. You have a chance to see a rare event. A Fire Drake is about to hatch in the nursery."

Gideon was so excited we could barely keep up with him. He whizzed this way and that, banking sharply to avoid the walls, then racing back and forth and banking again. It made me dizzy to watch and more and more I began to wonder at a technology that could give such unpredictable and convincing responses to an animated device.

"Gideon," Olivia called out to him. "What's a Fire Drake?"

"Oh, only the most famous Norse, fire

breathing dragon of all times. A lot of people think this famous human, Beowolf, slew the only one left, but a few survived in hiding in distant fjords and cliffs. As far as The Keeper knows, there are only two pairs left in the world," Gideon espoused.

"And the Zoo is breeding one of the pairs here?" my mom asked.

"Actually, no," Gideon answered sheepishly.

"But, you said you were hatching a Fire Drake egg," Olivia insisted.

"Yes, we are. The truth is, Grant and George and I sort of borrowed it. Late one night we were reading an article about how humans were removing Peregrine falcon eggs from nests, hatching them and returning them to the wild. So we figured, since baby Fire Drakes weren't surviving too well in the wild either, we'd follow suit."

"Bet you guys didn't get permission from The Keeper first, did you?" I taunted.

"No, we didn't," Gideon said, eyes downcast. "The Keeper castigated us quite severely, but now we'll see," he said, his face lighting up joyfully again. "The egg is actually hatching and a baby Fire Drake is going to be born, right here, at the Mt. Olympus Zoo."

By now we had arrived at a stone building with a soaring roof. Next to it were a series of different sized, stone cubicles with high walls. Gideon flew straight to one and perched on a wall, looking down into the cell. We walked around it until we found The Keeper and Dr. Lang standing by the gate to the stall. Sitting, cradled in a nest of what looked like real, gold coins was a lime green egg. The Keeper and Dr. Lang were whispering and motioned for us to be quiet. Every once in a while, Dr. Lang tiptoed in and listened to the egg with a stethoscope.

I stared at the egg, but didn't see anything happening until Olivia tapped me and pointed to a fine fracture-line that was climbing slowly up

the side of the egg. I heard a flap of wings and Grant landed in a high window in the cubicle and perched next to Gideon. Soon, another Gargoyle, who had to be George, joined them. All three Gargoyles had slap-stick-silly smiles on their faces.

The crack began to expand rapidly and Gideon sang out, "It's hatching, it's hatching," at which the egg crumpled into a pile of crumbled shell and a small still form sat in a bed of thick, grey fluid.

Dr. Lang sprang forward, grabbed the little form up and slapped it hard on the back. Grey fluid spewed from its mouth with a gargling sound and finally it squeaked. She slapped it more gently and a little steam escaped through its toothless gums. Finally she handed it to The Keeper who gently sponged it off and wrapped it in dry toweling. Turning to the three Gargoyles, he called, "Okay, Grant, Gideon, George, come down here and see your handiwork."

"Look at that complexion,"Grant said proudly.

"And those tiny, little claws," George said in awe.

"And that perfect tail," Gideon effused.

Dr. Lang shook her head. "They sound just like proud parents, don't they?"

She was absolutely right. Olivia walked over and pulled on the swaddling and looked in.

"He's so cute," she cooed, clicking her tongue and making baby sounds.

As for me, I picked up a coin and fingered it. Then, I bit it. I was sure it was real gold.

The baby suddenly hissed steam and Gideon flew up and whispered in my ear, "Drop it, buddy," which I did instantly.

"The Fire Drake's whole life consists of guarding a hoard of gold," The Keeper explained. "That hoard, in this case. Now let's leave this little guy and all his gold in the capable hands of Dr. Lang and see about the rest of your tour."

CHAPTER 6

Grant or George, I wasn't sure which, flapped up and whispered in The Keeper's ear.

"Excuse me, I'm terribly sorry, but I cannot accompany you. Once again, Gideon will be your guide. I'll send him immediately."

"It's beginning to look more and more like The Keeper is never going to be our guide," I said. "Dad, that stuff with the Fire Drake was pretty convincing, wouldn't you say?"

"They are very good, son. Very good. Amazing more people haven't discovered this place. I'll bet a year from now it's swarming with tourists."

"You know Harold, I get the impression that they are very selective about whom they let visit. So, I'll take that bet and if I win, the kids get to choose our next vacation."

"Way to go, Mom," I shouted.

"Ouch," Gideon said. "Keep it down Nicky, my boy. My head's a bit heavy today. I stayed up late. Might have known my services would be required right in the middle of my mid-morning rest schedule. The Keeper can't seem to remember that Gargoyles are nocturnal by nature. It's hopeless. So what realm should we start with today?"

"Gideon, why can't The Keeper take us around?" Olivia asked.

"Neighbor problems, but don't worry. I'm a better guide anyway. He's awfully dry. I'm much more fun. You can be assured of it. Now, which realm?"

"Underground," I chose quickly.

"Good choice, Nick, but then there isn't a bad choice either."

I was looking forward to underground tunnels and dimly lit passageways, but instead we stopped before a large sheet of glass, extending flat across the ground.

"Shoes off, everyone," Gideon chirped. "And on with the grippers, at least for anyone who can't fly."

Grippers proved to be bulky, heavily treaded shoes, much like snow tires.

"Now, move carefully out onto the glass and look down into the labyrinth below. This is a one way piece of glass, so that the animals are not disturbed by our presence. We worked very hard at designing a safe way to view these animals and it wasn't easy. We don't believe in cages, so this was a tough task," Gideon explained, taking a keeper-like pose.

"Which animals are kept here?" Mom asked.

"Wait, you'll see, you'll see," he said.

I stepped gingerly out onto the glass and found the grippers were quite effective. It was dark below. I could just make out a twisting pattern of caverns and passageways, but that was about all.

"It's hard to see anything," Dad remarked.

"Keep looking. Hopefully you'll see some animals. It used to be more fun when it was two way glass," Gideon sighed.

"Why did The Keeper change it?" I asked.

"I'd rather not say,"Gideon said a bit testily. I had a feeling it was not a happy memory.

"There," Olivia screeched, pointing.

"It looks like a panther," Dad said calmly.

"I suppose it does to you, but the Cherokee Indians say it's a Sacred Panther. They say it can see in complete darkness. It isn't as unusual as some of the animals down there, but at least you saw it."

"Uh, Gideon, is that dog down there supposed to be Cerberus?" Mom asked.

"Not 'supposed to be,' Mrs. Powers, it is. See the three heads with the manes of serpents? And the size, see how big?"

"Yes, but according to myth, he guards the gates to Hades and this isn't Hades."

"No, but he thinks it is. We tricked him a long time ago. He may have three heads, but he's not too smart."

Mom crouched down and stared at the three-headed dog for some minutes.

Just as she stood, Dad asked, "Is that a minotaur?"

It was a wonderful version. Probably nine or ten feet tall, black as pitch. It seemed to look towards where we walked as if it could see us. Raising its bull head and arms in a gesture of rage, it roared. We could feel the vibrations through the glass.

"Whoops, kind of mad today, he is. Let's try another realm, okay?" Gideon said.

"Why? He can't get to us, can he?" I asked.

"No, but I think he knows we're here, especially me. Sometimes I think he smells me right through the glass."

Taking the opportunity, I said, "Gideon, maybe you should bathe."

"That is not it," he said, his lower lip pouting-out. "He hates me is all."

"Why? What did you do to him?" I whispered into Gideon's ear.

51

He gave me a nasty look and flew off towards the courtyard. "Come on. If you humans can't move faster, I'll be stuck with you for a week before you see everything."

We scurried after him into another realm. Gideon flew ahead of us with no comments, obviously in a blue funk. Finally, we came to two, glass shafts that went straight up, and up, and up.

"These glass elevators were built for those of you who are wingless," he added pompously.

Looking up into the shafts, I wished I did have wings. They went so high they seemed to narrow before they ended. Stepping back and craning my neck, I could just make out what looked like slender walkways at the top.

"To insure your safety, you can do one of two things," Gideon continued. "You can wear a parachute pack. A bit bulky, in my opinion, to insure balance. Or, you can rely on the safety nets below. Frankly, I don't consider either to be satisfactory. I think everyone should be born with wings."

"Harold, maybe this isn't such a good choice," Mom said.

"Now, now, Mrs. Powers," Gideon

reassured her. "The walkway isn't very long and truly, we've never had anyone fall, really."

"How many people have you taken up there?" Mom asked.

"Well, it's a relatively new exhibit, so maybe six or seven."

"Oh, come on Martha. I'm sure it's safe or they couldn't get insurance," Dad urged, pushing us into the elevator.

"Insurance?" Gideon said as he flew in and the doors closed.

I quickly asked, "Gideon, is this an aviary or something?"

"You know Nick, birds are not the only ones who fly," Gideon answered disdainfully.

"I know. There are other things that fly. Mosquitoes, flies, bees, butterflies, bats, even gliding lizards and lemurs and such," I said.

"And?" Gideon insisted.

"Gargoyles," Olivia put in.

"Thank you, Olivia, but what else, Master Nicholas?" he went on.

"I don't know," I said shrugging.

"Well, Mr. Smart Guy, then you are in for a few surprises."

"Gideon, have you ever tried walking? Just to be sure it's as bad as you think?"

He ignored me. I winked at Olivia.

"What's the matter, Gideon, can't you walk?" I pursued the topic.

He ignored me again.

"Stop it, Nick," Mom instructed.

"Yeah, Nicky," O whispered. "This isn't a great place to make him mad. Wait til we're on solid ground again."

Actually, that seemed like good advice.

"Powers Family, I am obliged by a promise to The Keeper to suggest total quiet from here on out, in order to be able to observe those animals that roost here without drawing attention to yourselves, although there is one member of your family whom I would not mind having carried off."

Olivia giggled.

"Now the animals you will be looking for are the following: the Hipppogryph, originating in Europe, typically inhabits mountainous regions. It came to these mountains years before the Zoo was built and has remained since. Although its body is that of a horse, it has the wings, beak and claws of a Gryphon, which is half eagle, half lion. Unfortunately, as yet the Zoo has been unable to obtain a Gryphon.

"Mixcoatl is the Aztec cloud serpent. Not to be missed, it is the last of its kind anywhere. It is not to be annoyed or teased as it isn't as gentle as I am," Gideon said eyeing me. "The Perytons used to hover over Atlantis in flocks. We are fortunate to have one pair."

"The lost city of Atlantis?" my father asked, his disbelief clear.

"Yes," Gideon answered. "That Atlantis, Mr. Powers. The only Atlantis there ever was in fact or fiction. Anyway, Perytons are green, plumed bird-deer. They're very dramatic, especially since they cast the shadows of men instead of deer. But, be careful, they can also be fierce!"

"Gideon, if everything flies up here, what about birds? Don't you have any mythical birds?" Olivia asked.

"Birds, firds! How come everyone thinks of birds when they think of flying? What about Assyrian Winged Bulls and Chinese Celestial Dogs or flying horses like Skinfaxi, that Teutonic horse whose mane spreads the gorgeous, golden streaks of light across the sky that all you humans 'oooh' and 'ahhh' over? But no, humans only ask about birds," Gideon raved.

"Or airplanes," I said.

"Birds," Olivia insisted.

"Yeah, yeah, we've got birds. We've got Yata Garusa, a Japanese, three-legged crow; Poua-Kai, a Maori eagle-type bird and Feng, the three legged, Chinese Phoenix by which humans are always stupefied. They think it's so beautiful and so sweet how lovey-dovey he and his mate are. The Feng just reeks of Eternal Love, with a capital 'E' and a capital 'L'."

"Yuck," I said.

"Now, that's better, Nicholas. I like that reaction, my man," Gideon agreed, but I saw Mom and Dad smiling at each other the way they did when they thought they knew something I didn't.

"Okay, slow and easy now, and keep quiet," Gideon said softly.

We clung to the rope handles along the narrow walkway that circled the mountain side. Feeling eerily detached from the earth, trying not to look down, we were buzzed by something big that dived at us from overhead. By the time I looked up, it was a spot in the distance. Then it was a spot in the distance that was turning and heading back. I held my breath as it landed on a rock about two hundred feet away. It still looked big, very big. I couldn't quite decide if it was a snake or a dragon. I tried to remember the list that Gideon had mouthed out and finally decided it was Mixcoatl because little clouds were floating

around it and Mixcoatl was a cloud dragon.

As if in slow motion, Gideon gestured for us to move on. Mixcoatl seemed to ignore us, but I could see that caution was a good idea.

I let my breath out as Gideon led us up a side ramp and pointed into a crevice. A pair of incredibly beauteous, three-legged birds were fussing over an egg. Mom and Dad were smiling and holding hands as they watched, and Gideon was shaking his head.

"Fooey," suddenly exploded out of the little Gargoyle into the perfectly quiet air. He clamped a wing over his head as he realized he had broken the rule of silence. One of the birds burst out of the crevice in an upward soar and dived back at us. Gideon ducked and we all followed suit as it swooped over us and landed just above the crack in the rocks, shimmering wings spread, plumage extended for full effect.

We scurried quickly back to the main walkway, Gideon with an embarrassed look on his face. We rounded a curve to find the walkway virtually blocked by a large, eagle-like bird perched across it. It cocked its head at Gideon and watched him as if he were prey. Gideon sank to the walkway and froze. The bird fluttered a little closer and my stomach sank as it landed on Gideon's head. I watched its claws, waiting for them to sink into his little body, but they didn't. Instead, I heard a distinctly stone-like sound as it pecked his head. Gideon had turned to stone.

The minutes stretched out forever until the perturbed Poua-Kai called a high, wide squeal and wheeled off into the sky, vanishing into the sun's glare.

Olivia rushed to Gideon, tapping him gently. He opened one eye and then the other and grinned. Olivia instinctively hugged him until he looked like he would gag. He pushed her away and flapped off as if nothing had happened. We never saw the Perytons or Yata Garusa. We made the mistake of arousing the Hippogryph. It roared down onto the walkway, shaking and tearing at it as we clung to the ropes and Gideon tried to distract it, shouting, "Shoo, Shoo!"

It spun around and as it turned, it's tail flipped Olivia over the rope and she began to fall. Mom screamed as Olivia tumbled into space, apparently scaring the Hipppogryph because it finally flew off, leaving us to watch Olivia plummet down and down. She was twenty feet from the ground and closing when a magnificent horse flew underneath her. She desperately grabbed his mane and clung to it for dear life.

The horse sent sparks of gold flying behind it, streaking the sky with radiance. It flew around, tossing its head, finally landing, shaking its head

again and dislodging its unwanted and unexpected passenger.

By the time we got down to Olivia she was alone, shaking and more than willing to have Dad carry her. When we got into the courtyard we noticed that if she waved her hands they left streaks of golden color hanging in the air.

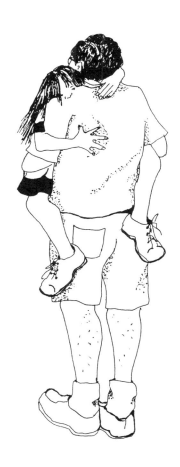

CHAPTER 7

It was only ten in the morning, but it seemed we'd been up forever. We must have looked pretty listless because Gideon seemed concerned.

"Come on, perk up. Listen, let me suggest a short excursion on the way through the Woodlands. If we hurry, I can promise you a nice snack and a cup of tea."

"Gideon, maybe we should just go back to our room," Mom said, holding Olivia tightly.

"Oh please, Mrs. Powers. I promise you nothing like that has ever happened before. And besides, you can't go to your room because it is in the process of being cleaned."

"Great," Dad groaned. "When will the room be ready."

"It'll be at least an hour, so tea it is?" Gideon asked.

Mom and Dad nodded wearily and we trundled after our flighty friend.

"Olivia, are you okay?" I asked. She didn't answer. She was terribly quiet, gently waving her hands and watching little, golden rays slide off them. "Olivia," I tried again. "Why do we listen to a robotic creature like Gideon as if he is real?"

"Cause he is real, Nicky. He's just as real as you or me," she said with absolute certainty and waved her hand in a golden trail.

Gideon's little detour took us through a field and onto a trail through a patch of seedling trees, up a steep hill onto a stony ridge above a small drop off on the side of the mountain. So, there we were, dead tired and walking even more while Gideon flew along whistling some medieval sounding melody.

I was getting more and more resentful when he announced, "Here we are," and ducked into a good sized cave.

Dad went up and tapped on the side of the cave and peered in. Some extensive spider webs were visible and it smelled mildly damp.

"It's real," Dad announced.

"Who would serve tea in a cave like this?" Mom asked.

"Who indeed?" Gideon asked, popping back out. "Why are you loitering out here while the tea is inside getting cold. It's terribly rude you know, when everyone is waiting on you. Now, hurry, hurry, hurry."

"Come on," Olivia said, leading the way. "Gideon, hold my hand. It's dark in here."

To my surprise, the Gargoyle dropped to the ground and they trundled, hand in hand, through the entrance to the cave. Of course, we

all followed along. The entrance was tunnel-like, only wide enough for two abreast, so I brought up the rear. It was a bit damp and definitely dark, but Olivia left a glowing trail that we followed. Not too far into the cave a soft glimmer of light appeared and shortly the cave opened into a large room, full of candles and Gargoyles.

"Goodness gracious, Gideon. Humans certainly are slow. Come on, come on, it's tea time right now," an old Gargoyle scolded. She wasn't wrinkled, but her stone was stained and pocked and she walked with an elderly gait.

"So sorry, Grandmother Gertrude. It's a bit touchy dealing with humans."

He swung around and glared at us, motioning us to sit on rocks arranged around a series of flattened boulders running the length of the room.

As we sat, a bunch of little Gargoyles waddled in bearing trays of steaming cups and large pots with twisted spouts. The cups were laid out along the table and there was a sound like a hoard of flapping crows. The table was overwhelmed with Gargoyles. A particularly tiny guy pulled on my arm and asked for a hand up.

"Hi," he said solemnly. "I'm Gerald."

"Nicholas," I introduced myself. "How many Gargoyles live here?"

He gestured around the table. "We've been here a long time, much longer than The Keeper. Once we numbered in the thousands. Now we are merely one-hundred-and-twenty-one, not counting the old hermits who roam the back hills."

"Does Gideon always bring the tourists here?"

"No, you're an experiment. Granny Gertrude and a few of the other elders have refused to associate with humans. They have continued to view them as monstrosities. We finally managed to get them to agree to give a human family a chance and Gideon recommended you."

"He did?"

"Grace," Granny Gertrude proclaimed at that moment, bringing everyone to instant silence. "If it please, whoever be, give us rocks and stones and bees. Thank whoever made these things, blessed be she or he."

"Dig in," Gerald said, as a tray of honey-covered rocks was passed our way.

I was wondering what the proper etiquette was for a Gargoylian tea when Gerald picked up a rock, popped it in his mouth and crunched the whole thing down, licking his fingers as he finished.

"Gerald, humans can't consume rocks. The best I can do is suck off the honey."

"Oh dear, we had no idea, no idea," he cried in a distressed tone.

"Don't worry, but I didn't want to offend anyone."

"Oh dear." He jumped down and trundled over to Granny Gertrude, holding a whispered conversation. Back he came. "She says not to worry. Just enjoy the honey."

"Thanks," I said.

Dad looked at me and winked. I wondered what he thought now? Either, someone was a multi-multi-billionaire who spent, but didn't advertise, and didn't care if he made anything off this place, or we had stumbled onto the biggest discovery of all time. Only we hadn't exactly stumbled on it. We had purchased tickets to it through a travel agent.

"Tea-Time-News-Time," a smallish Gargoyle sang out. "Who wants to go first?"

"Well, something got into our beehives again. Looks like a bear. Did a good job cleaning out the honey."

"Nothing we can do. Bears have a right to honey, too," Granny Gertrude pronounced. "Gideon, what news of The Keeper's problems with the town?"

Gideon stood up and looked at us for a minute. "I don't know if I should discuss this in front of our guests," he said somberly.

"Oh, quit dramatizing. Spit it out Gideon," Granny Gertrude insisted.

"Very well. All I can say is that rumors are dangerous. Some tourist who passed briefly through the Zoo has accused The Keeper of harboring vampires of all things. Vampires are

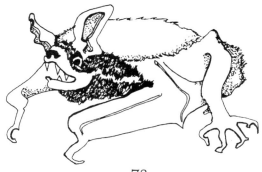

clearly mythological creatures! Absolutely no grounds for believing in them! Anyway, the town won't admit to believing such nonsense, but all of a sudden they are asking a lot of questions, want a complete inspection of the facility and have indicated they generally don't trust us. The Keeper is tactfully trying to keep them at bay, but a suit to close us down has been mentioned. They claim we never got a zoning permit, the meatheads."

"Did we?" an older Gargoyle asked.

"I don't know. I never knew there was such a thing. Humans make up more rules than any other creature on Earth," Gideon replied, clearly miffed.

"So, what is The Keeper going to do?" Gerald asked next to me.

Gideon shrugged. "He hasn't told me. He doesn't confide in me at all. I only knew this much because I, uh, well, listened at the door."

"Gideon," Granny Gertrude reprimanded him. "Aren't you ever going to learn to respect other people's privacy?"

"Then how would I learn anything interesting to tell you?" Gideon asked happily.

"Granny Gertrude always says that and Gideon always answers the same way. It's a tradition," Gerald giggled.

Dad cleared this throat. "Has anyone suggested to the town that the Zoo is a great way to boost their economy. Think of the motels and franchises they could have."

All the Gargoyles looked at him silently. Finally an old male who had spoken before said, "Mr. Powers, we are not a tourist resort. Despite your obvious disbelief in our existence, we are in fact a culture of some complexity and antiquity. Unfortunately, The Keeper felt obligated to issue free invitations to people with children in an attempt to keep the world educated. We Gargoyles tried repeatedly to tell him that this was a risky business, but The Keeper was very determined. Our opposition was to no avail and now we can only hope it has not been a fatal mistake that brings tragedy down on us all."

"You are a very eloquent speaker, Sir," my dad replied, "but I'm sure it will all work out. I am most sorry if I have offended any of you."

"It's all right, Mr. Powers. For humans, you and your family have been presentable," Gideon said.

"Gideon, if the Gargoyles are so opposed to tourists, why did they invite us to tea?" Mom asked him.

"Curiosity? Some of us elders wondered if you were as bad as we thought," Granny Gertrude said a bit sheepishly.

"Well," I asked, "how bad were we?"

"Not too loathsome," Gerald said.

There was a general round of consent. "But, they're awfully picky eaters," a particularly pock-marked Gargoyle added. "Licking the honey off and leaving the rocks!"

"Sorry," Olivia said looking guiltily at the honey-less rock on her plate.

"You wasted your rock?" a small Gargoyle accused with a nasty tone in his voice.

"You know, Gideon, I think we should leave now, before this conversation gets out of hand," Dad said stiffly.

"Thank you so much for your hospitality," Mom said, addressing Granny Gertrude.

"Bye," Olivia said glumly, waving gold.

CHAPTER 8

"Sorry," Gideon said. "I didn't mean for it to end like that."

"I wasn't trying to be rude," Olivia said. "It's not as if I could have eaten that rock if I'd wanted to."

Gideon offered her his hand, but she shook her head and refused. After a bit he said again, "Please, I'm truly sorry."

None of us answered.

"Well, you might as well see the Woodlands now anyway and then we can go back."

I walked next to Dad who was so quiet I knew he was really, really mad. He always got angry if someone upset Olivia.

"Dad," I said as quietly as I could. "Why are we so mad at a bunch of Gargoyles. You know, imaginary, stone creatures from Medieval architecture. They're not even real."

"Hey," Gideon glared, but Dad patted me on the shoulder and began to whistle. As for me, I winked privately at Gideon, who blinked for a minute and began humming along with Dad.

The Woodlands proved to be the biggest realm at the Zoo. Basically it was an unaltered, mountain habitat. Birds sang out and we spotted numerous familiar species of animals. Grey and red squirrels jumped acrobatically from limb to limb. The ground was strewn with salmon colored, coral mushrooms and ferns of all sorts. Tiny, native orchids grew at the bases of trees and soft carpets of pine needles covered paths. Except for the Gargoyle accompanying us, we could have been in any pristine woods, anywhere.

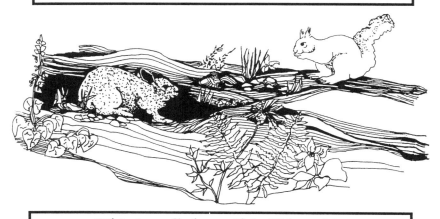

"This is really beautiful, Gideon," Mom said softly.

"Quite right, Mrs. Powers. This was our easiest habitat to establish. And it's full of fascinating creatures, as well. For instance," he said, flying to the top of an extremely high tree, "here

is the nest of a cinnamon bird, the Cinomolgus. His nest is made of cinnamon sticks, one of my favorite treats," he added, reaching into the nest which we could barely make out from below.

"GIDEON! Down from there, now," The Keeper boomed, breaking the silence as he came up behind us. "How many times do I have to warn you to leave that bird alone?"

"Aw, why do you always come along just at the wrong moment," Gideon complained, but descended quickly.

"Gideon, I do not have time for this. I came merely to deliver these ear plugs to you and the Powers family. When you hear me whistle three times, all of you, quickly and firmly plug your ears with these. Wait ten minutes before removing them and then continue about your business."

"Sure, Boss," Gideon said.

Olivia was peering around The Keeper at a mouse-sized, grey animal with huge eyes and wings, who was fixedly returning her stare.

"Ah," said The Keeper, "a Volkh."

He gently plucked up the creature and held it cupped in one of his hands.

"Isn't that a sugar glider?" Dad asked. "What's a sugar glider doing in these mountains?"

"Watch," The Keeper said.

Even as he spoke, the creature seemed to shimmer and The Keeper was holding a chipmunk. Shimmer again and a beautiful monarch butterfly was poised there; shimmer again, a lovely goldfinch flitted off his hands and into the tree tops.

"A Volkh is a Slavic shape-shifter, as you could observe. It's known for its magical powers and is usually difficult to spot unless it shifts into an animal inappropriate to its environment."

"Such as a sugar glider," Dad suggested.

"Yes," The Keeper said. "Now I must go. Remember to listen for the three whistles."

"Okay, okay," Gideon answered The Keeper in the same tone I talked to Dad.

"What else might we see Gideon?" Olivia asked.

"That," Gideon pointed. "It's a Hippocerf."

"It looks like a horse," Olivia said.

"No, a deer, O," I corrected.

"It looks like both," Mom stated.

"Right, Mrs. Powers. That is the problem with a Hippocerf. It can't make up its mind about what it is. It can't make up its mind about much. Sometimes it stands around trying for hours. It's one animal you can count on seeing easily in our Woodlands."

"Oh, looky. I know what that is. It's a Unicorn," Olivia cried.

"They both are," Gideon said, pointing out a second animal. "The 'deer' with the short horn is a Chi Lyn from China. This is the first time I've seen one. It only comes out when a great man is born. I wonder who just got born?"

"I guess they don't come out too often then," Dad commented.

"You're showing your cynicism, dear," Mom said.

"Be very quiet. Both Unicorns are very, very shy," Gideon whispered.

We watched until they ran off without making a single sound or breaking a single twig.

Olivia sighed, "There really are Unicorns."

"Olivia," Dad admonished. "Don't start believing so much of this."

Olivia didn't argue. She knew better. Instead she winked at me.

The afternoon was wearing on and I was hungry, but we had hardly seen any of the Woodland creatures. Gideon told us to watch for a Salamander that breathed fire. He claimed it could even walk through fire without being burned. It sounded unlikely to me, but Mom said

it was a common European legend. So, I was searching the ground for a lizard when Gideon shouted, "There!"

I thought he had found the Salamander, but he was pointing at what looked like a Panther, not a Salamander. It was a dark color and flames blazed from its head, back and legs. It scorched the ground it walked on, leaving a burned odor in the air, but nothing caught fire.

"What was that?" Dad exclaimed, as it slinked off.

"A Polynesian Panther."

"And what is that?" Mom asked, pointing up into a tree.

I squinted until I saw what she had seen. It looked more or less like a possum, except its tail was too long and I was pretty sure it had wings.

"Where?" Gideon asked.

"There," Mom pointed.

"Where?" Dad and Olivia chorused.

"There," I pointed.

"Oh, that," Gideon said. "That's a Nuddu Waighai, first cousin to the Virginia possum, commonly known to the Australian Aborigine. It's said it attacks hunters, but so far there haven't been any hunters to test it on."

"Listen Gideon, it's getting pretty late. I think we should head back," Dad decided.

"Yes, I suppose, but not before I show you a Bird of Paradise."

"Do you know where this bird is?" Mom asked a bit skeptically.

"Sure, it's always hanging in the same place. It hangs upside down by its tail feathers from a tree because it has no feet or wings."

"Poor thing," Olivia said.

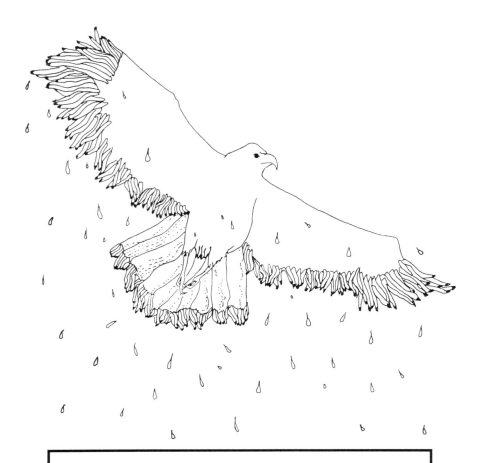

"It's perfectly happy and if you're lucky,
Olivia, you'll find a couple of its feathers lying
around. There it is," Gideon said, pointing into a
stand of beech trees.

We could see it from afar, so brilliant was
its plumage. It was about the size of a goose and
it sang out the sweetest, clearest note I had ever
heard. We stood transfixed for several moments
until a shadow passed over us. We looked up into
the wing span of a giant Eagle.

"Oh, it's Oshadagae," Gideon exclaimed. "He's early today. He brings the dew every evening. The Bird of Paradise sings when he comes because she eats the dew."

The shadow passed over us again and a fine mist of water rained gently down, bringing a sweet smell with it

"I like that bird," Gideon said. "It's a native of America. The Iroquois Indians have known of it for generations."

Finally, we turned and headed back to the courtyard. It was close to dinner time, but all I wanted was a bed. We were trudging slowly along, none of us talking when we heard the three whistles and saw The Keeper. Gideon frantically helped us stuff in our ear plugs. The Keeper began tugging wildly on a plant, pulling and heaving, but to no avail. Dad walked up and gestured. The two of them bent over and yanked, then pulled again and again. Up came the plant and as it pulled out of the ground, even through the earplugs, I could hear something of a piercing scream. The Keeper whipped out a shiny length of silky fabric and quickly wrapped up what looked like a little man hanging from the leaves. Dad scratched his head as he walked back to us.

While we unplugged our ears, The Keeper rapidly double-timed it back towards the courtyard with his bundle.

"I'll be," Dad said. "The root of that plant was a perfect, little man as white as snow. As soon as The Keeper wrapped it in silk, it seemed to be quite content. Never saw anything like that. Not anything."

"Me either, and I thought I knew everything there was to know about these woods," Gideon admitted.

"You mean there is actually something you haven't wormed out of The Keeper?" Dad said.

"I should know what that was, but I can't quite remember," Mom mused, ignoring Dad and Gideon.

"I'm tired," Olivia complained. "Let's go back."

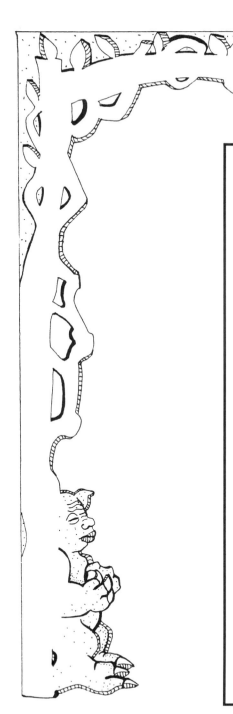

CHAPTER 9

The courtyard was jammed full of people when we got there. At first I thought a bus load of tourists had pulled into the Zoo for a tour. A large man who looked very hot and bothered was haranguing Dr. Lang, who was the only Zoo official visible.

"No, you can't tour the Zoo. You don't have an invitation or permission," I heard Dr. Lang proclaim in a firm voice.

I turned to ask Gideon what was going on, but he had frozen, statue-like against the door frame of the Woodland Realm, indistinguishable as anything more than sculptural decoration.

"Hey," another heavy-boned man squeezed into a pin-striped suit addressed us. I noticed that his pants were too short, as he said antagonistically, "Who are you?"

"We're the Powers family," Dad answered. "I'm Harold, my wife Martha, and Nick and Olivia. Might I ask who you are?"

"We are a committee from the town . What are you folks doing here?" another man asked more calmly.

"Why, taking an extended tour of the zoo, of course," Mom answered promptly.

"And?"

"And what? We're having the time of our lives," Dad said with a smile.

"That right?" the man asked. "Have you seen or noticed anything weird?"

At that moment I was really glad Gideon was a snoop and we had gone to tea at the cave.

Dad played it straight and innocent.

"Weird? No, I don't think so. I'd say

fascinating, unusual maybe, but nothing threatening, if that's what you mean."

"Just exactly what have you seen?" a mousey looking woman with a shrill voice asked.

"Well, there's an awful lot to see. Nick, what did you like best?" Dad said, throwing it to me.

"Uh, let me see. A sugar glider, a wild horse with an incredibly beautiful mane," I said looking at Olivia, who had carefully stuck her hands into the pockets of her sun dress. "A couple of panthers, some pretty rare eagles." I made it sound so average I surprised myself.

"Any bats or wolves?" the pin-striped man asked.

"Nope, not yet, but we've got several environments left to tour," Dad admitted. "Personally, I'm quite fond of wolves. I think it's a shame what man has done to them."

"It's fun here," Olivia chimed in her sweetest, little girl voice. "I'm having the best summer vacation ever."

Not that that was saying much, but she was right. It was great.

Look," my dad said. "What's this all about, anyway? Everyone here has been lovely. The food is great, the rooms are clean, Dr. Lang takes great care of the animals. There's no abuse or anything. The price is reasonable, so what's up?"

"Forget it. I'm going home," the calm man said, striding off towards the gates. Soon the rest of the crowd followed him, except for one, small, dark-eyed, intense man.

"Tell your boss Dr. Lang, this isn't over just because he hired these folks here to lie for him," he said pointing at us. He left slowly looking around at the courtyard and taking a few snapshots with a palm sized camera. I watched him, his hair slicked back into a steep widow's peak, graying at the sideburns and I thought he looked vampirish himself. I wondered if he was searching for relatives.

Dad turned to talk to Dr. Lang, but she had already slipped away and Gideon had vanished as well. "Shoot, I wanted some explanations," he said.

"Me too," I said.

"I'm sleepy," Olivia said, pointing with a glowing finger towards our rooms.

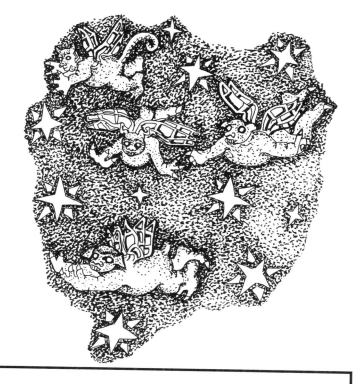

CHAPTER 10

By nine that night Olivia was sunk deep into the down covers, sound asleep. Mom was brushing her hair out when The Keeper knocked lightly at the door, with a large, torch-style flashlight tucked under a billowing sleeve.

"The Gargoyles and I are going to tour our newest realm. It is not yet open to visitors, but we wanted to thank you for helping us deflect the town's fury this afternoon by inviting you along."

Mom said no, she would stay with Olivia, but encouraged Dad and me to go, so we slipped

back into our clothes and followed The Keeper
out.

It was a true summer night of stars. They
filled the sky, not like pin pricks, but like large,
tangible jewels that looked close enough to be
plucked from the black night. A group of rowdy
Gargoyles flew in and out of my line of vision,
breaking the view of the sky. In the dark they
seemed a bit ominous, like grey shadows that
shouldn't have been there.

Gideon landed on my shoulder, his dark
eyes casting the true, reddish-orange glow of a
night creature.

"I hope you like snow, young Nick. We're
headed to the Arctic, land of ice and eternal
night," he chattered loudly, right into my ear.

"It's quite a new exhibit and so somewhat
sparsely inhabited," The Keeper said. "Several of
the animals can be dangerous, so we are forced
to view them from behind walls."

In this case, the walls were made of
multiple panes of thick glass, each pane
surrounded by reinforced steel, so that it was like
looking through a many paned, clear, stained-
glass window, except higher and free standing.

The area the wall enclosed was filled with thick snow and boulders of frozen ice.

The Keeper told us in a very soft voice, "The Arctic Mole originates in China. It won't come out in the day because it dies if sunlight touches it. It spends its life tunneling and . . . There! Look. See?"

"It looks like an over-sized walrus," I said in surprise.

"Yes, it does, Nicholas, but walruses don't burrow, so the Chinese call it a mole. A bit misleading in some ways, but appropriate in others."

"Oh, oh," one of the Gargoyles began to chirrup. "Look out, look out, look out Mole!"

In fact, the mole made an unexpectedly graceful dive into its burrow in time to avoid a Grizzly-sized, semi-bear that was pounding down on it.

"The Bird-Bear is here by default, so to speak," The Keeper said unhappily. "It's really far too aggressive for our environments. It's an Icelandic animal. Unfortunately, for both him and us, the humans of its home regions have expanded their cities to the point where there was no place left for it to go. It was poaching livestock and being actively hunted and I was asked, perhaps begged is a better word, to house it."

The Keeper sighed as he watched the beast scrape at the Mole's tunnel until it collapsed. With the Mole no longer of interest, it noticed us

on the other side of the glass. It charged the wall, scratching down it with heavy talons. It pressed its bear snout against the glass in a snarl, and spread a set of ineffectual wings that could not possibly have lifted its great bulk. It was ugly, no question, and nasty, and left gouges in the glass, and I was really happy when it gave up and vanished behind a pile of snow.

The Keeper was shaking his head and Gideon was just plain shaking and saying, "Big mistake. I don't like that guy. I just don't like him."

Neither did I.

We followed the wall for quite a way until a medium-sized dragon flew up on the other side and cocked its head at us, almost like a friendly dog. It had round, dark eyes and was covered in transparent, silver scales. It sat calmly observing us until one of the Gargoyles suddenly stretched its wings. Startled, the dragon brought its head back and blew. The whole glass was consumed in fog, which almost instantly froze over into ice, obscuring everything from further viewing.

"Godfrey," The Keeper turned to a Gargoyle and scolded. "How many times do I have to tell you, you must be absolutely still when a wild creature is near. Do you see what you caused just now?"

"What kind of dragon was that?" I asked.

"An Eskimo dragon called Palraujuk."

"I thought dragons breathed fire?"

"Not this one. He breathes frigid air and I'm afraid he has frozen the whole wall, so we might as well return to the main building. Drat," The Keeper fumed in frustration.

"If The Keeper could breathe fire right now, he would," Gideon giggled into my ear.

The Keeper calmed down and dropped back to walk next to us. The small hoard of glowing Gargoyle eyes was eerie in the starlit night.

"Sorry this proved to be so disappointing," he apologized. "The Gargoyles always make things a bit unpredictable."

"I noticed they are a bit temperamental," Dad agreed, "but all in all, it was still fascinating."

"By the way," I interrupted, "how is the little Fire Drake doing?"

The Keeper shook his head. "Not too well,

I'm afraid. So far, Dr. Lang hasn't been able to stabilize his condition."

"Gee, that's too bad," I said. "Olivia is going to be upset."

The Keeper sighed and shook his head. "He might have been better off in the wild." He sighed again. "In any case, I think you will be able to finish seeing the rest of the realms by tomorrow evening. I hope you'll join us for a grand feast before you leave. Perhaps you should plan on spending tomorrow night as well?"

"That would be great," Dad said. "By the way, I was wondering, how are you planning to deal with the town?"

"I've an idea or two, but let me ask you and Nicholas something, Mr. Powers. What do you make of us, of all this?"

"Well, uh, I'm not sure, to tell the truth."

"Nicholas?"

"It's real, all right. I mean, I know it's impossible, but here it is. I mean, here I am with a Gargoyle on my shoulder. But, I have to tell you, I'd never tell anyone, because no one would believe me. And, when I write my annual 'what-

did-you-do-over-the-summer' essay, I am going
to lie."

"And you, Mr. Powers? What are your
choices as to what we are?" The Keeper persisted.

"Look, I'm a realist. I work hard at a job
that is secure, but repetitive. Every summer I try
my best to do something different, something
interesting. So far, this is the best summer, that
much I'll give you. But, I'm still a realist and I
keep wondering who finances this place and how
you've managed to make it so convincing. The
issues with the town make me even more
curious. Why would a whole town feel threatened
enough by the Zoo to want to close it down? I
guess, I personally think you're an elaborate
hoax, but fun, and I'm willing to leave a little
room for wondering."

The Keeper smiled and patted Dad on the
back. "You're a good, normal man, Mr. Powers.
Stay that way, but be sure to leave that little
crack for wondering, okay?"

The Gargoyles turned and flew off into the
hills and we walked back in silence and the un-
broken darkness.

CHAPTER 11

"We had a real problem replicating a plains environment here on a mountain. You know, getting a flat, open surface wasn't so easy. So, you have to use a little imagination here and there. Fortunately, the animals seem happy enough."

"What should we look for here, Gideon?" Olivia wanted to know.

"Let me see. We've got a couple of lion-like creatures from various parts of the world. We'll try and spot them first. In this realm we'll be walking through enclosed paths with portholes for viewing, for the sake of safety. Although we wish you could experience the animals closer at hand, the truth is, some of the mythical beasts are not that cute and cuddly. One time, one of the lion-like guys tried gnashing his teeth on my cousin, Galvin. It left quite a number of permanent scratches in the finish of his stone that no one has been able to sand or grind out. It was quite painful, so even Gargoyles are wary of these beasts."

"Do you have a Nemean Lion?" Mom asked.

"Sure, it looks like a big lion with a black mane. Not too exciting unless you're being mauled by it."

"Look there," Dad pointed. "What on Earth is that?"

"A Parandrus. Be very still and quiet,"

Gideon whispered, slowly folding down his wings. "It comes from Ethiopia. See, it's got the head of an Ibex, the horns of a Reindeer and a shaggy coat like a bear. If you watch carefully, I'll show you something really surprising about it."

The Parandrus had wandered quite close. Suddenly, Gideon shot straight up above the wall, flapping and screeching hideously. The poor beast was totally startled, leapt into the air and ran awkwardly to a nearby clump of bushes, where it stopped and stood stark still. A second later it had almost vanished as its color changed to a dark green, matching the bushes perfectly.

"A mythical chameleon," I said happily.

However, Olivia turned to Gideon angrily and said, "Meany! Why did you do that?"

"Oh drat, Olivia. How else was I going to show you what it could do?"

"I bet The Keeper doesn't know you do that," she said.

"No, probably not," Mom agreed.

"Olivia," I said, trying to distract her from glaring at Gideon. "Look what's coming our way."

A big eared, wrinkled faced, little creature was poking around in the grass, slowly wandering towards us. Its face looked like something between a pug-nosed dog and a bat. It had a bristle of fur instead of a tail and from the top of its head grew what looked like a huge, shiny ruby.

"That's a Carbuncle," Gideon said quietly. He searched in a little bag he was carrying until he found corn kernels which he handed to us saying, "You can feed it if you put your hand up to the little door in the wall. It'll nibble out of your hand."

"Ooooh, it tickles," Olivia giggled.

"A Carbuncle comes from South America. It's very rare, but the natives claim that the jewel is magical and very medicinal. Unfortunately, we

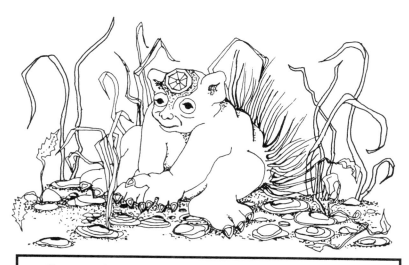

will never know because The Keeper won't let us explore the possibility."

"How could you explore it, Gideon," Mom asked, "without removing the ruby?"

"That's the problem, Mrs. Powers, exactly the problem. Got any ideas?"

"You're incorrigible, Gideon," she said.

"He's cute," I said as he ate the corn from my fingers. "I'd like one of these for a pet."

"No," Dad and Mom said at the same time. "You know the rule, no pets. Kids are enough."

"You don't need to worry, Mr. and Mrs. Powers. There have never been more than a handful of Carbuncles in the world, so no one can have one for a pet," Gideon said.

"Too bad," I said as Gideon closed the little feed door.

"Well, here comes another strange one," Dad said.

"Is that a Ping-Feng?" Mom asked.

"Sure is," Gideon confirmed.

"They are famous in Chinese mythology," Mom explained.

The silly thing was a fat, black pig with a head at both ends of its body. It ran awkwardly, as each head tried to be the front end. Finally, one gave in and ran backwards.

"Dumb, dumb, dumb. It'll never learn," Gideon said in disgust.

"Unlike Gargolyes, who always listen to instructions?" I asked.

"Nicholas, you are a pain. I won't miss you one little bit when you leave tomorrow."

"Then you don't want to be pen pals?" I asked sarcastically.

"Pen pals? You mean, write to each other?" Gideon said, obviously surprised.

"Me too," Olivia added.

"Sure, why not? I've always wanted to get mail," Gideon said.

"Great!" Olivia shouted. "Isn't that great, Nicky?"

"Sure," I said a bit dully. I hated writing letters and what did you say to a Gargoyle?

Gideon was smiling and humming to himself over the prospect of getting mail when he shouted out, "Oh lucky day!"

I thought he was so happy because we were going to be pen pals, but he added, "It's a Yale!"

"It's a black antelope. Nice dye job, Gideon," Dad was saying when the Yale's antlers swiveled around in a three-hundred-sixty degree arc at the approach of something big and ugly.

"Oh, oh, oh. Crocotta! How'd she get out of her cage. Oh, oh!" Gideon screeched. "Hurry, Nicholas. See that gong over there. Wang it hard and keep doing it while I try and distract her."

I ran to the gong, trying to watch Gideon at the same time. He was taking flying dives at the Crocotta. The Yale had vanished in one swift leap and somewhere, something was crowing like a deep, thunderous rooster. Olivia had her hands over her ears and Dad was screaming something at Gideon. All the while, I hammered the gong.

"Gideon, stop! The poor thing. Quit harassing it immediately," The Keeper boomed as he came hobbling up as quickly as possible, followed by two younger keepers who promptly threw a large net over the Crocotta. It struggled weakly as they quickly gathered it up, but the crowing continued.

"Now look at what you've done, Gideon. You've awakened the Cock of Dawn and who knows when he'll stop crowing and how many roosters around the world think it's dawn because they hear him and so are crowing at the wrong time of day as well. What is the matter with you? The poor Crocotta doesn't want to be around any other creatures, including and especially excitable Gargoyles. Someone merely left the gate to its habitat open, and it innocently wandered out for a walk."

"But the Yale was in danger," Gideon said.

"Gideon," The Keeper said loudly and none too happily. "I know you find the Crocotta ugly, but it isn't its fault. You'd be ugly too if you were a cross between a hyena and a lion, but the

Crocotta would be sorely pressed to catch or eat a Yale. Yales are nimble and have the defense of rotating horns, while the Crocotta, if you will, is slow and hampered in movement by a rigid spine. The fact is that it is impossible for it to sneak up on any animal because it smells so dreadful. Now please, use a little common sense next time. Between the town and the little Fire Drake, I don't have time for this."

The Keeper stamped off and Gideon slumped into a dejected heap.

"Woe is me. Goofed up again."

"Aw, come on Gideon. I goof up all the time. I'm always getting bawled out for one thing or another," I said.

It didn't help. I even thought I saw something wet, like a tear, drip out of his eye, except it was grey. Olivia tried funny faces. Even Dad tried a pat on the back, but Gideon stayed in a heap until an animal literally crawled over him as if he was a rock in the trail.

"Oh great, now the Rompo is loose. Look at the thing, will you? It's really stupid looking with that rabbit face topped off by human ears," Gideon said glumly.

"Personally, I think the Zoo went too far when it thought up this animal. A weasel's body, badger's feet in front and bear's in the back and that tail! Extraordinary is the kindest description I can come up with," Dad said with a laugh.

Gideon didn't even retort. He just continued to sit listlessly with his head bowed.

"Oh, come on Gideon. What kind of animal do you claim the Rompo is?" I asked.

"It's a scavenger, found in Africa and India," Gideon said dejectedly.

"Well, it's the best proof yet that all this is make believe," Dad said.

"How can you say that, Mr. Powers? There it is, the living proof," Gideon said petulantly, sticking his feet out in front of himself.

"Gideon, if you don't quit being sad, I'm going to tickle your feet," Olivia threatened.

He popped up and scrubbed at his face with his fists and said without much enthusiasm, "Let's go see what else we can find."

In the background I could still hear the Cock of Dawn, but the crowing was softer now.

We followed the path around the enclosure until Gideon stopped.

"Usually the Cameleopardel is wandering here, eating leaves and stuff off the trees. There it is."

Off in the distance was a tallish animal resembling a camel without a hump. It sported two backwards curving horns and its body was covered in spots.

"It's an herbivore," Gideon announced. "Know what that means, Nick?"

"It's a vegetarian. Hey Gideon, what are you?" I asked. "A rockivore?"

"Ha, ha. Real funny, Nick."

"Well, don't they have a classification for Gargoyles, Gideon?"

He actually stuck his tongue out at me. It was slimy grey, too.

"I've had enough for one day. I'm going back and The Keeper will have to find someone else to take you around. I'm done, done, done," he said jumping up and down. "No more humans, never, ever again. Not for me."

He trundled off, waddling a step, stamping his feet, then flying a few steps, stamping his wings, if that was possible.

"It hasn't been his day," Mom sighed turning to face me. "And really Nicholas, you made it worse. When are you going to learn to think of other peoples' feelings?"

"Martha," Dad intervened. "Gideon isn't real. He's a Gargoyle. G-A-R-G-O-Y-L-E. Remember, they're not real."

"Is that so, Harold? Are you sure?"

She stamped off just behind Gideon, with all too similar body language. Unfortunately for me, I agreed with Mom. I couldn't look at Dad at all. My eyes were glued to Gideon's angry, little, slumped figure.

CHAPTER 12

"But Gideon, it's only three more realms," my mom pleaded. "Really, Olivia and I are so fond of you. Please be our guide."

He eyed me and Dad angrily. "Sorry, Mrs. Powers. George can take you."

"Gideon, I can tell you lots of secrets about Nicky," Olivia offered a little too happily.

"Hey O, that's not fair!" I shouted.

"Tough, Nicky. You shouldn't have hurt Gideon's feelings."

The Keeper trounced in looking anxious and muttering loudly.

"People! My goodness, do they really think they can make themselves disbelieve by threatening us with a court order? What's so awful about true myths? As for you Gideon, I don't have the time or energy to deal with sensitive Gargoyles. George is already busy and I am going to have to hire a lawyer unless my Mandrake comes through soon and brings us good fortune. So you have to continue with the Powers and that is that."

Turning, without awaiting a response from Gideon, he hurried through the outer gates.

"Harold, you're a lawyer," my mother pointed out.

"I'm on vacation, Martha, trying to get away from being a lawyer."

"But think of the fun of defending the Zoo, Harold."

"Martha, I . . . well, uh . . ."

"Come on, Dad. Be our hero. You only half-disbelieve and you do like this place, and The Keeper wouldn't have to try to explain everything to a stranger," I said excitedly.

"Harold," Mom said. "This is your opportunity to put your doubts to rest, or confirm your suspicions of chicanery."

"Go for it, Big Guy," Gideon shouted unexpectedly.

Dad threw up his hands and double stepped off to look for The Keeper as we all burst out laughing.

"So, your Dad is a lawyer? Maybe the Mandrake is working after all," Gideon mused.

"This Mandrake everyone keeps mentioning, was he that little man The Keeper and Harold pulled up in the woods?" Mom asked curiously.

"Yep. The Keeper says if you treat him nicely he is supposed to bring good fortune. Maybe in this day and age he's brought it indirectly, by having Mr. Powers turn out to be a lawyer."

"Maybe," Mom agreed. "And maybe he's bringing your dad a little luck and fun, too," she whispered to me.

"I don't know, Mom, but I know something is making Dad act differently," I said back.

"Or you're seeing him anew," she suggested.

"Well," I said quickly turning my attention to Gideon, "I guess you're stuck with us."

"I truly am," he said kicking at a rock, but he didn't really seem upset anymore.

"Can I bring a camera?" Olivia asked. "So Daddy won't miss everything."

"Sure, but no flash. We don't want to scare any animals."

"Me too?" I asked.

"Sure, sure Nicholas, but any trouble and it is confiscated."

"How come you didn't say that to Olivia, Gideon?"

"Because I play favorites," Gideon said, gleefully flying into the air. "Now move it, hurry, hurry, hurry."

First stop after we got our cameras was the Swamp. Ramps meandered through watery plant life and great blue herons soared and dove, silhouetted against the sky, reminiscent in shape and movement of ancient Pterodactyls. Anywhere else that would have been a sight, but it paled when the Hydra raised its heads. Olivia and I snapped picture after picture until it dove below the surface of the swamp.

"Boy!" I shouted. "That was great. How many heads does it have?"

"Both the first Hydra back in Greece and this one started with nine, but so many people have chopped at this particular Hydra's heads, it now has more. This is the last Hydra in the whole world. You know who Hercules was, don't you? He killed the first one."

"But, I don't get it. How can chopping off its heads give it more heads instead of less?

"Because, Nick," Mom said, "every time someone cut off one of its heads, it grew back two or three more to replace the one it lost."

"A very useful trick," Gideon commented.

"He smelled funny," Olivia said. "Is he a dragon?"

"Naw," Gideon said. "A serpent, Olivia. Quite a bit different. He is Serpens hydraeus."

"Looky," Olivia cried.

Crawling up onto the bank came an animal with the face of a frog, the body of a lizard and forelegs that looked almost like arms.

"Lacertus botrax," Gideon announced. "Amusing and harmless. It has almost no protection other than how quick it is. See," he pointed

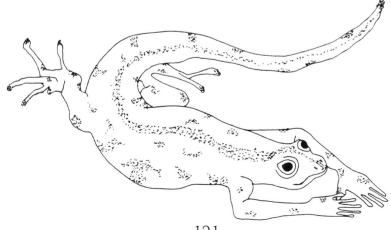

as it slithered swiftly into the water. "There is also Lacertus saura which goes blind when it gets really old. Then it finds a hole in a wall that faces east, stretches out to the rising sun and poof, it can see again like magic. But, almost no one sees the Lacertus saura."

"The Botrax was too fast for my camera," Olivia complained.

"Well, try the next guy on for size," Gideon said, flapping down the walkways, which seemed to be rising higher and higher. "We're going up for safety. And now you can see why. See him? Morou-Ngou."

I was so taken aback, I almost forgot to take a photo. The creature had the walk and spotted body of a leopard, but it was dripping wet and its paws were webbed.

"What?" Mom sputtered.

"It's a fierce, African carnivore: Morou-Ngou, Panthera aquaticus. It's very, very fast on land as well as in the water. Don't ever go in a boat in a lake or swamp reputed to contain a Morou-Ngou. Big mistake," Gideon pronounced, shaking his head sadly. "The Morou-Ngou once tipped over a boat with Garreth Gargoyle in it.

Garreth sank straight to the bottom and was never heard of again."

"Did the Morou-Ngou eat him?" Olivia asked, her eyes big.

"No, I doubt it. I don't think Morou-Ngous can digest stone. It's just that Gargoyles can't swim. They sink like a rock, you know."

"Why was he in a boat?" Mom asked a bit skeptically.

"A foolish, foolish Gargoyle. He took a dare from his brother Gimmy to ride in a boat. Oh, sad day. Sad, sad, sad day," Gideon moaned dramatically.

The Morou-Ngou glared up at us and snarled a clearly cat sound, then gracefully and with speed dove into a deep part of the swamp.

"Usually, Morou-Ngous live in a lake, but our lake was inhabited by too many defenseless creatures, so we put the Morou-Ngou in a deep swamp. Do you see that big, black, humpy thing over there?" Gideon continued. "That's a Catoblepas, usually found in the Ethiopian mud flats, where he wallows and wallows happily, filthy his whole life. Yuck! But, maybe it's just as well, because The Keeper claims if he gets energetic and stares at you, and you see his eyes, bang, you drop dead," he emphasized.

"What's he look like close up?" I asked.

"They say he's a scaly buffalo, with boar's tusks and little wings, and an overly large, heavy head, but since I don't want to drop dead and turn to stone forever, which is death to a Gargoyle by the way, I'm not going to find out."

"Gideon," I asked, "are all the Gargoyles

adorning city buildings dead?"

"Oh yes, oh yes. Absolutely. Sitting there forever stone. A Gargoyle's worst nightmare," He said in an agitated state.

"Awesome," I said without meaning to. "The cities are Gargoyle graveyards."

"Nicholas, where are your manners?" Mom warned as I clamped my mouth shut and Gideon stared open-mouthed at me, his grey tongue resting loosely on his lip.

"Aren't there any nice animals in the swamp?" Olivia asked.

It took him a few minutes to answer. "A couple. Down the walk, Olivia," he finally said without looking at me, "is a Caiman. He's not too nice, but he can't kill you by looking at you. He looks like a crocodile, except he is slimmer and has human hands with bird talons for finger-nails. He's fairly common in South America."

"We already saw a Chinese Crocodile at another zoo," Olivia said, "and a Komodo Dragon. I didn't like the Komodo, but Nicky did."

"They are ugly, aren't they."

She nodded her agreement. The Caiman was half buried in mud, so we couldn't tell if it really had human hands, but Olivia took its picture anyway.

We walked on, with Gideon taking a few reckless dives out over the swampy water, even though Mom tried to stop him. Without warning an incredible animal sprang from the water, covering Gideon with a spray from its trunk and then joining him in twists and dives through the air. First we were awe struck, then howling with laughter as the boxy, little Gargoyle and the creature performed an air ballet that reminded me of an elephant and ostrich dance. Gideon had a broad, happy smile plastered over his face.

"What is that thing, Mommy?" Olivia asked.

"I have absolutely no idea," Mom replied. It looked half elephant and half fish. Whatever it was, Gideon and it were having the time of their lives, until the beast dove back under water, creating a wave that momentarily engulfed Gideon.

The silly Gargoyle finally rejoined us, shaking water every which way and announced breathlessly, "That's a Makara from India. It can fly, swim and walk on dry earth. Can't exactly be classified, but he's a great buddy of mine. Let's go, I'm famished." He shook one more time and drenched me as he flapped off.

CHAPTER 13

Not too many people or Gargoyles showed up for lunch, but Gideon made up for it, eating four extra portions, finishing off with a gigantic, fudge-covered rock, which he munched with great relish.

"I can't afford to become a light-weight. Gargoyles have been known to fade away into mere slivers of themselves," he said between gulps and crunches.

Mom and Olivia and I just nodded.

Dad and The Keeper sat with their heads together at the far end of the table. Every once in a while I caught a drift of conversation.

"How did you obtain the land for the Zoo?" Then, a buzz of words. "Does anyone own the land?" Another buzz. "In all the years you've been here, the town never protested before?"

And so it went, with Dad mainly asking the questions. Finally, he stood up and said loudly enough for us to hear clearly, "Look, you're going to have to decide how you want to approach this. How are you going to present yourselves? Are you an institution of higher research, an amusement park, a straight zoo or what?"

"How about a conservation organization?" Mom suggested.

"Conservation of what, Martha?" Dad asked, turning towards her.

"Mythology," she answered readily. "Maybe the Zoo could be an educational organization devoted to the preservation of myths. It could hook up with schools and make learning about other cultures and mythologies truly real and meaningful. Our kids have surely learned a lot here, and loved every minute of it."

"That's a great idea, Mom. The Zoo could be the OOMC, the Organization of Mythological Conservation," I said.

"They may have something here," Dad said, scratching his head.

"And Harold, no one would have to know whether or not the beasts are real. It doesn't really matter, does it?" Mom pointed out.

"I suppose school children would like it here," The Keeper said, smiling at Gideon.

"Wait a minute. WAIT JUST ONE MINUTE! WAIT ONE DARN MINUTE," Gideon screeched. "Does this mean hordes of Nicholases running all over, cause if so, I'm going to quit."

"Quit what, Gideon?" The Keeper asked trying to keep a straight face. "I never hired you, you know."

"That's true. You couldn't pay me enough to work here, but it hasn't kept you, has it, from Shanghaiing me into being tour guide and baby sitter to impolite humans."

"You mean me?" Olivia asked, pulling on his wing.

"Well, no, not you, Olivia. You're pretty nice," he said, looking a bit confused.

"Gideon," my dad put in. "I hope this idea works, because it's the only good idea we've had, and if it doesn't work, then the Zoo and you, too, may be out of a home."

"Aren't there any other choices?" Gideon pleaded.

"We'd be happy to entertain any you have," The Keeper said politely.

"How about not giving any more tours," Gideon suggested.

"Too late for that, the damage is done, my friend," The Keeper admitted apologetically.

"Let the Ihuaivulu destroy the town."

"Gideon," The Keeper admonished, shaking his head.

"Well, why not? They deserve it."

"Gideon!"

"Okay, okay, then how about a magic spell?"

"Magic spell? Be realistic, Gideon."

"I was, I thought," Gideon muttered dejectedly.

The Keeper threw up his hands. "So much for Gargoylian ideas. Come along, Mr. Powers."

Off they went as Gideon kicked the wall with a heavy thump. "I thought the Ihuaivulu was a great idea. I can see the headlines in my mind: NATURAL DISASTER BURIES MOUNTAIN TOWN UNDER LAVA!"

"What is an Ihuaivulu?" Mom interjected into his tirade.

"Come on, I might as well show him to you. He's in the Mountain Realm, which I'm supposed to show you anyway."

Gideon was very pensive as we rambled along. He'd flitter a few feet, then descend and kick at this stone or that, mumbling about how unappreciated he was, complaining about how The Keeper took human advice over his, a friend of many years standing, then flap a few feet and kick another stone, even waddling on his stubby legs for a space without realizing he was walking.

"Gideon," Mom finally tried approaching him. "The Keeper is in a real predicament. He has to find a reasonable way to deal with some unreasonable humans. If the Gargoyles were being unreasonable, I'm sure he'd turn to you, but for cantankerous humans, he needs human advice. Isn't it you who are always saying what dopes humans are? I think maybe the town is proving you right, quite right."

"Hey," he said, his face brightening. "You're right. I mean, you're right that I was right. I mean about humans, I was right. They are idiots . . . uh, with a few exceptions," he said looking sheepishly at Mom. "But, I suppose you're right as well about The Keeper needing an expert on humans. Whoops," he said as he flew into a small, four-footed dragon and got knocked flat.

"Ooof," he exclaimed as he sat there with a surprised look on his face. The dragon nuzzled

him and Gideon laughed. "This is a Puk. He comes from the Baltic. He pretty much has free reign of the zoo. You never know where he'll turn up, but if he comes to your home, he brings gifts," Gideon said, falling over as the Puk nuzzled him again.

"Almost too domesticated," Gideon laughed, finally extricating himself. "Come on quickly before he knocks me over again, but be careful. There are a bunch of pretty fearsome creatures in here. Mainly they ignore tourists, which makes me suspect that tourists aren't too tasty, possibly very tough or even poisonous to Mythical Beasts," he said rather condescendingly. "Now then, if you do see On-Niont, you win a prize. Nobody, except The Keeper, has ever seen On-Niont."

"Then how does anyone know what to look for?" Mom asked.

"The Huron Indians left descriptions. They called it a big serpent with a horn that can pierce a mountain."

"What do we win if we spot it?"

"A year's supply of honeyed rocks."

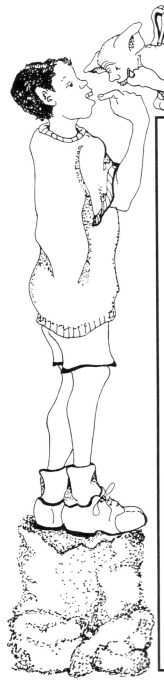

"Oh great," I said, rolling my eyes. "How about just the honey?"

"I guess that would be okay, but I can't see why any-one would pass up the rocks."

"Gideon," I said, opening my mouth. "Look at these teeth. Are they the teeth of a rock muncher?"

"I guess not. Poor you. Humans have awfully little teeth," he said seriously, peer-ing into my mouth.

"Look out," Olivia called, as a stormy looking creature swooped by us on the run. "That's a funny looking animal," she added.

"Well, don't laugh too

soon," Mom said. "That's a Chimera and as I recall, it brings storms with it. Look at the sky. It's really clouding over fast."

"Stupid thing. Maybe there is still time to finish the mountain before it storms," Gideon remarked while we snapped pictures of the three-headed Chimera. It was a silly looking thing, with the mane and body of a lion, legs of a goat and the tail of a dragon stuck on its rear end. I guess its body made some sort of sense since its heads were those of a lion, goat and dragon.

"Come on, Nick, those clouds are awfully black," Mom called.

I hurried to catch them. "No time for Ihuaivulu, but you can see him from here. The seven-headed guy, who breathes lava like a volcano, even looks a bit like a mountain."

"I see him," I said, thinking I was just as glad we weren't going any closer.

"You should have seen the crate that he was shipped in from South America and he was a lot smaller back then. No matter what happens, the town is stuck with him, because he's too big now to crate back up," Gideon remarked gleefully, with a big, contented smile. "Now hurry.

The Keeper won't forgive me if I don't show you the Persian Simurgh. It's unlike any other bird in the world. Actually, only half bird. The other half is mammal, although I can't imagine why. Mammals are so, well, pasty. Anyway, it suckles its young like a mammal and its feathers can heal almost any disease or wound, but the part I like best is it hates snakes. So, I keep hoping someday I'll see a great battle."

"Well, not today," I said as thunder roared. "We'd better make a run for it, or a fly-for-it, as the case may be."

"Nick is right," Mom said.

"Can rocks attract lightening?" Olivia asked, looking at Gideon as we broke into a run.

"No," Gideon said, "but I still don't stay out in a Chimera instigated storm if I can help it."

The rain came pouring down in sheets before we got back. It was so thick I couldn't see through it. Gideon herded us like blind cows into the courtyard and up the stairs to our rooms. We stood in the doorway, soaked and dripping all over the floor. Dad and The Keeper were having coffee in front of a roaring fire. We wrapped up in blankets and sipped hot chocolate while the storm howled outside, making the day blacker than dusk.

"You must have run into the Chimera," The Keeper remarked. "I'm sorry. It should really be caged when visitors are here, but it is quite hard to both locate and catch. Where is Gideon?"

"He flew off with Garth or George or somebody. He said he didn't like lightning storms. They make him want to hide under a bed."

"That's probably where he is," The Keeper smiled, "so maybe your dad and I can get some work done."

"How are things going, anyway?" Mom asked.

Dad shrugged and threw up his hands. "We've got a basic perspective, which is a start. What happens partly depends on what the town does. If they merely go to the County Zoning

Commission, then we get our best shot. If they decide to sue and go to court, they can ask for all kinds of information in discovery. Then the fun would really begin. We don't want that. What we do want is to get the Zoo listed as an educational, non-profit institution. If we can get ourselves listed as an educational institution fast enough, then maybe we'll be able to convince the Zoning Board to issue us a permit. That might end all this, provided the land is owned by the county or the state and isn't held privately. And, that I'll have to find out by taking a trip to the County Seat. If we end up in discovery and the town gets to ask for any background information they want, we're in big, big trouble because the Zoo is going to be vulnerable to a lot of prying, some nosey snooping and possibly a lot of superstitious, nonsensical prejudice."

"And that could be dangerous, I'm afraid," The Keeper said softly.

"You know, you could just close up and turn everything off for a while, until this all blew over. Why do you keep acting like you don't have any choices?" Dad asked a bit nervously.

The Keeper just smiled sadly at Dad.

"I don't think we'll be leaving tomorrow,

Martha. I'd like to stay as long as we can and try to see this thing through, or at least get it under control for the Zoo. Is that okay?" Dad asked.

"Sure Dad, that's great," I butted in.

"It's fine with me too, Harold, but maybe you could use some extra manpower. I could compile some educational literature and brochures," Mom offered.

"What a wonderful idea, Mrs. Powers."

"Could I help Dr. Lang with the baby beasts?" Olivia asked.

"I'm sure Dr. Lang would welcome the company and the help, Olivia. She really has her hands full, especially since the baby Fire Drake is so sick. How about you, Nicholas?" The Keeper asked.

"I don't know yet. Maybe I could take some more photos for Mom to use?"

"Wonderful. A family like you might even change Gideon's opinion of humans," The Keeper said, tapping his blue fingernails on his coffee cup.

"What made Gideon feel this way about humans?" Mom asked.

"I think he resents the fact that humans proved to be real instead of creatures of Gargoylian mythology as he had been raised to believe."

"You're kidding," I exclaimed. "That's pretty whacky."

"Well, not if you're a Gargoyle. They even have tales of how people capture Gargoyles in human cities and cause their deaths by em-bedding them into buildings for decoration. Of course, that's all nonsense."

I thought of all the mythical things modern humans thought were nonsense and hoped The Keeper was right.

"What else do these mythical-human-beasts do?" I asked curiously.

"Oh, it's a wonderful set of tales. See if you can find one Gamial G. Gargoyle to recount them to you, Nicholas. You'll love them."

"Hear that O?" I asked, but she was asleep in a ball near the fire, looking very small and wet.

CHAPTER 13

"Mommy, do you think the gold will ever wear off?" Olivia asked waving her hands in wild patterns through the air. "I hope not. Then I'll never forget this place and Daddy will have to admit that everything here is truly real."

"I don't know, sweetie."

"If it doesn't, you'll be famous, O," I called from the bed. "Hey Dad, how far is it to the town?"

"A few miles, I guess. Why, Nick?

"Uh, I don't know. I just wondered."

"One of the things I have to check on is how close the Zoo really is to the town limits and if traffic to the Zoo would impact on the town. The Keeper doesn't think there's a road directly to the town. If he's right, that's to our advantage, but he's not sure because he's never gone into town."

"Dad," I said quietly. "You seem so happy. You like trying to solve all this, don't you?"

He seemed startled or maybe a little

embarassed. "Why yes, I do Nick. Now why don't you run along? I've got work to do."

Mom was busy making phone calls from The Keeper's office. As far as I could tell there was only one phone in the whole zoo. There were no televisions I had seen, no computers and no mail. Federal Express had appeared a few times at the gates, but that was it. I wondered how Gideon and I would write each other when we left. O was going to help Dr. Lang feed the baby animals.

"Do you think the baby Fire Drake is going to die, Nicky?"

"I hope not, O, but it doesn't sound too good."

"I'm not going to let him die Nicky. I'm not!" she insisted and ran off to Dr. Lang.

That left me on my own, so I went looking for Gideon. I found him engaged in a game of Chinese Checkers with Grant, while George kibitzed and offered both of them advice.

"Gideon?"

"What? Oh, it's you, Nicholas. What is it?"

"Uh, can I ask you a favor?"

"A favor, no. It's almost time for a nap, something I haven't had since you came. No favors today."

"But, Gideon, it could be really important."

"To whom?"

"To the Zoo. To The Keeper's plans. Please, won't you at least listen to me?"

"Oh drat. You are the peskiest boy. Sorry Grant."

"Are you abdicating?" Grant asked, raising an eyebrow.

"No, I'm not."

"Then you can't quit."

"I'm not quitting. I'm just calling a recess."

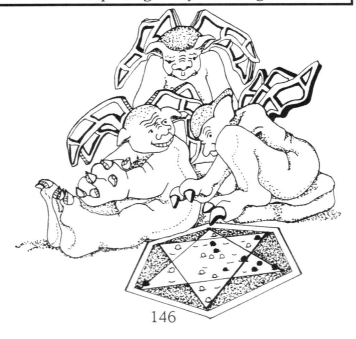

"You can't do that. You know the rules. You lose by default if you leave the playing field."

"It's an emergency."

"Then you lose."

"I did not lose."

"If you quit, you lose."

"Guys," I yelled. "You sound like a pair of six year olds. It's only a game."

"Yep, a game Gideon lost," Grant cackled.

I grabbed Gideon and pulled before it all started again.

"Gideon, I need your help," I pleaded.

"All right, already. My, but you are a nuisance. If it weren't for the Zoo, I'd never speak to you again."

I nodded. "How old are you guys, anyway?"

"All I'll say in that regard is, Gargoyles live a very long time. Now what do you want?"

"I need you to help me get to town."

"What? Why? No, no! The Keeper will drown me in the lake."

"Gideon, it's okay. I'm a human kid. Human kids are supposed to go off and do dumb things like this. I'm willing to risk my dad's wrath. See, no one ever really notices kids, or they pretend not to because it's easier than dealing with whatever it is the kids are doing. All kids know this. It's one reason they try all sorts of stuff they shouldn't. So, I'll be able to snoop without anyone asking anything. I bet we could find out some important stuff."

"Not me, Nicholas. You're asking the wrong creature. One look at me and the town will bomb the Zoo. I'm a Gargoyle, remember? A myth, an impossibility, an implausibility."

"Okay, just take me within a half a mile and point me in the right direction. Please, it'll be fine."

"How are you going to get back?"

"You'll wait for me?"

"I was afraid you were going to say that. It's a five mile hike. Are you up to it?"

"Sure, I'm in good shape," I said, righting my slouchy posture to prove it.

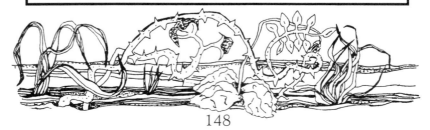

"And nobody knows you're going?"

"No," I answered sheepishly, but honestly.

A big smile broke out across his face. "I love to break the rules. Let's do it, Nick, old boy."

Although the woods were beautiful, I couldn't enjoy them because I had to watch where I was going. Since Gideon flew everywhere, he didn't think about the dangers wild-rose brambles or poison ivy presented to a pasty fleshed boy. He flew right over them or even through them without a scratch or a worry. I sipped at my canteen as I picked out the safest path and Gideon razzed me about being too careful.

"Hey, Gideon, where did that tourist come up with the idea of vampires?"

"Well now, let's see. I think it was in September when she came," he said and stopped.

"So?"

"And we were reading about Halloween," he said and stopped again.

"Oh, oh. Is this sort of like the Peregrine falcon story? Maybe you shouldn't read?"

"Well, maybe we shouldn't, but The Keeper is always encouraging us to educate ourselves about the human world, which was all we were doing. Anyway, Grant has this kid sister, Geraldine, whom he really finds irritating. She's always nagging him about one thing or another. 'You should tidy your part of the cave, Grant; you should settle down and stop fooling around with that Gideon, he's a trouble maker,' and stuff like that," Gideon said in what was clearly a high, nasal imitation of Geraldine.

"Let me guess. He decided to scare her by pretending to be a vampire."

"Right."

"Did it work?"

"No, but it wasn't our fault. It should have worked. Geraldine deserved it. She is such a ninny, almost as bad as humans."

"Oh really," I said calmly, not rising to the bait.

"Anyway, this tourist who was visiting was about five foot two inches, big ear rings and broadly lipsticked, red mouth that never stopped running. We weren't expecting to be seen at midnight on a starless night, so we weren't too cautious. The Chimera had been out and it was clouding over for a bad storm. It was the perfect night for a scare. We pilfered a pair of plastic, vampire teeth from a kid and I helped Grant cram them into his mouth. He grinned at me, teeth dripping out, and flapped off to find Geraldine. I went back to my perch and dozed off until I heard a piercing scream. Lightning struck. A louder scream. Grant swooped glumly back to where I was. Clutched in his hand was the shattered remnant of the fake vampire teeth.

"Below, we saw The Keeper scurrying along, and even from that high up we could hear him muttering and ranting about pesky Gargoyles.

"'What happened?' I asked Grant.

"'Oh, it was dreadful. That red-lipped woman!' he exclaimed shuttering. 'I saw her wandering about the courtyard and forgetting I had in the teeth, I flew up to see what she was doing out at midnight. I scared her, that was the first scream. The second was when the lightning struck, illuminating the sky and my face. She saw the teeth and hauled off and punched me in the mouth. Her fist shattered my teeth and she groaned, grabbing her hand, which I hope she broke. I'm so mad! I'll never have such a good chance to scare Geraldine again,' Grant had said morosely.

"He stayed mad all that night and every time it had thundered, he had kicked the parapets and stumped his toes, which had made him howl. I guess that finished the lady off, plus even though her hand wasn't broken she still had teeth marks in her fingers when she left in a huff the next morning. Stupid, stupid, big-mouthed woman," Gideon said disgustedly.

"Boy, I'll bet The Keeper was mad that time."

"Actually, at the time he chuckled, but none of us dreamed of what was coming. Humans are so unpredictable. I have to admit, Grant must have been a shock to that lady in the middle of the night, eyes glowing, mouth oozing with teeth, but still she just went nuts, starting all those exaggerated, inaccurate rumors. And Grant never forgave her for breaking his teeth."

CHAPTER 14

We came out of the woods by the side of a paved road.

"This is as far as I go, kiddo. You're on your own. See that old stone wall, I'll wait for you over there by it, but if some old cow or dog comes sniffing me, I'm gone. I don't like domesticated animals. They smell."

"Thanks Gideon. I'll see you in a couple of hours."

I started off down the road. A boy on a bike whizzed by and a car beeped at me. I felt disconnected, as if I was dreaming. I stumped into town, kicking at a pebble, thinking how alien it felt to be there.

I took a deep breath and meandered down the street, practically bumping into a gang of kids heading into an ice cream shop. I fished around in my pockets and found enough money for a cone.

As I waited in line, I asked the kid ahead of me, "What do you think about the Zoo up on the mountain? I heard it was pretty neat."

"I don't know anything about it. Ain't ever been there, but my old man sure is up tight about it."

"He is? Why?"

"Aw, he says there's something bad going on up there."

"Really? What?" I asked, but he just shrugged.

"Vampires," a girl behind me said.

"Vampires? You've got to be kidding. Adults don't believe in vampires. Kids don't even believe in them," I exclaimed innocently.

"True, but adults are weird," a lanky boy said.

"Goofy," I suggested. "Who'd believe such nonsense?"

"Well, Preacher Martin told Gertrude Jones that she was panicking. It made Mrs. Jones real mad. She said she has it on good faith from a lady she met who had been to the Zoo."

"You mean that whacky, tourist lady?" I asked. "Mrs. Jones didn't even know her til she stopped here for all of one night," I said, acting like I knew this Mrs. Jones really well.

"Aw, Gertrude Jones has been silly as long as my pa can remember," the lanky boy said. "My pa says it's all a waste of energy, a lot of furor over nothing."

"Mine too, and he's the town lawyer," a small, freckled kid said.

"Your dad doesn't think he has a case?" I asked, trying not to seem too interested.

"Aw, he says all we've got is hearsay. Said a judge would throw it out. That lady with the big, red mouth, she left without even leaving her name and address."

"But," said a girl in a halter top, "I sure would like to see that zoo."

"Why?" the lanky kid asked. "I didn't know you liked animals, Virginia."

"I don't particularly, but Bill and I were out one night and . . ."

"Hey Virginia, Daddy told you to stay away from Bill. He's bad news," a younger girl interrupted.

"Be quiet, Pint. This wasn't recently. Bill and I were up there and we saw something."

"What?"

"We couldn't tell. It was too dark."

"Oh, there aren't no vampires. You were just spooked cause you thought someone was going to catch you together," Pint said.

"I never said vampires. I said we saw something."

"Go on, Virginia, you're nuts," the first kid said.

I slid away while they were arguing and ran smack, bang into the fat man from up at the Zoo.

"Slow down there, son," he said. "Do I know you?"

"Uh, I don't think so, Sir," I said very politely, licking at my cone, trying to hide my face as much as I could.

"Seems like I do."

I shrugged and walked away as calmly as I could. As soon as I was out of sight, I ran. I ran, walked, ran again until I got to the wall. I heard a dog fussing and barking, and there was Gideon up a tree, a dog running about the base, wildly baying.

"About time," he hissed. "Aren't you ever on time?"

"Gideon, we never made a time. I thought you were going to leave if a dog came."

"Nicholas, the point was, you were suppose to be back before a dog came."

"I was?"

"Of course. Don't you understand anything you're told?"

"Come on, Gideon. Let's go. Goodbye, dog," I said, thinking that Gargoylian logic was a bit warped.

The dog barked and nipped at us for a while, until someone whistled for it. Reluctantly it left, but not without a final, throaty growl.

"Dogs don't like Gargoyles,"Gideon pointed out. "I hope it was worth it, young Nicholas."

"It was. Wait until I tell Dad and The Keeper."

"Tell me first."

"Oh, no. I know you. You'd blab before I got to tell."

"Nick, how could you think that of me?"

"You're a natural snoop, Gideon, and you can't keep a secret and you can't wait to tell all to everyone."

"And to think, I waited for you and let that dog harass me so you could get home with your precious news."

"True," I admitted. "Well, it's good news. Real good news, but that's all I'll tell right now."

"Hmmmp," Gideon said, and wouldn't speak to me until we saw the gates.

Then he flew off and I could hear him yelling, "GOOD NEWS, GOOD NEWS," as loud and as fast as he could.

CHAPTER 15

Dad finally quit yelling at me for going AWOL. I got bawled out a lot at home for doing stuff kids do, but it sounded worse here because it echoed back at me over and over off the stone walls.

"Dad," I appealed, "are you through because I really did find out something good."

"Nicholas, you shouldn't have been in the town at all," he said for the millionth time, and it echoed around for the one-hundred-millionth.

"Dad, the town doesn't have any witnesses. None. Nada," I offered.

He stopped short. "No witnesses? Really? Well now!" he said with a smile.

"Who told you this, Nicholas?" The Keeper asked.

"A bunch of kids in an ice cream parlor were talking about it, but one of them was the son of the town's attorney, and he said his dad doesn't think they have a case. Isn't that great, Dad?"

"Yes, it is Nicholas."

"So, am I still grounded?"

"Absolutely. Just because it turned out all right doesn't mean you should have gone off like that. It was dangerous."

"I know. You've told me that, but how else could we have found out about it?"

"That isn't the point," Mom said. "This time it worked out okay, but it isn't worth the chance that it won't some time. Do you understand, Nicky?"

I nodded as The Keeper turned to Gideon and said, "And Gideon, you were completely irresponsible. If I were your father, I would ground you as well. Fortunately for you, you are not my son."

"It's okay by me too, that I'm not your son," Gideon said completely unabashed. "I've got a question, Mr. Powers. Even if they had a witness, who would have believed her, especially that old, blabber-mouthed tourist?"

"Probably no one, but they might have been able to go to court, and if The Keeper had answered all the discovery questions as if all this was real, now that might have opened a can of worms."

"Well, now we don't have to worry about it, do we Dad, thanks to Gideon and me," I said hopefully.

"Maybe not, if information gleaned from kids in an ice cream shop turns out to be reliable. In any case, we need to proceed quickly to establish the Zoo as an educational facility. Perhaps we should take some photos of you kids with the animals, so we can build a portfolio of information slanted to an educational presentation. Also, we should join a few organizations to establish our credibility."

"We already belong to the MBWF," Gideon cheerily reminded us.

"Ah, I think Dad meant some normal groups," I pointed out.

"Normal? You mean human," Gideon accused.

"Gideon," Mom said gently. "Humans, perhaps unfortunately in your view, dominate the world now."

"And threaten it," Gideon added testily.

"Perhaps, but if you want to survive you have to deal with reality."

"Humpf!"

I started to laugh.

"Nicholas, Gideon's discomfort is not funny."

"It's not that, Mom. Don't you see. Here we are, four humans, formerly considered stable pillars of the community, trying to convince a Gargoyle he should deal with reality so we can save a zoo full of myths."

There was a moment of silence until even Gideon was smiling.

Dad and The Keeper went off to The Keeper's inner sanctum and Gideon excused himself for a nap. I looked around for Olivia, but she had already slipped away.

"Where's Olivia, Mom?" I asked when she hadn't returned in a half-hour and I was beginning to wonder what to do with myself.

"With Dr. Lang. I think they are trying to feed the baby Fire Drake. Oh my, Olivia had asked me to tell you to join them. Dr. Lang was going to give you two a tour of the nursery."

"Oh boy, Mom! Is it okay? I mean, am I allowed to since I'm grounded?"

"I suppose, but don't get into any more trouble and take the camera, Nick. We could use a few nice photographs for our brochures."

"Sure, Mom. See you," I said, hurrying out the door.

I got to the courtyard in time to see a clutch of Gargoyles take flight as if startled. Grant was left sitting on top of the table.

"Hey Nick, what's up?" he asked in a tone I recognized as that I used when I was caught with my hand in the cookie jar, so to speak.

"I was going to ask you that, Grant?"

"Not much."

"What was that all about?" I asked, indicating the departing Gargoyles.

"Not much. Gargoyles do a lot of congregating about a lot of nothing. See you," he said, taking wing as quickly as he could.

I hurried on, worried about being late. Olivia was standing back to back with the Fire Drake while Dr. Lang measured to see who was taller.

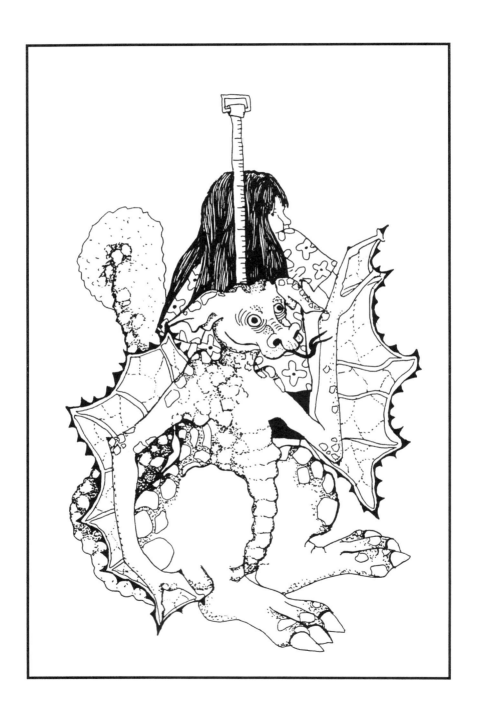

"He's growing fast," Olivia said.

"But not gaining weight and that worries me."

"Maybe that's normal for Fire Drakes," I suggested as I joined them.

"Maybe, but its out of most biological norms, even most mythical norms. The Gargoyles are very concerned because he hasn't yet breathed any fire. Their intent has always been to return him to his parents, but they aren't sure he'd survive and neither am I. I've wondered if the adults would accept a Fire Drake that can't breathe fire? I'm even more concerned that he keeps gagging up fluid and eats almost nothing," Dr. Lang mused.

"What does The Keeper say?" I asked.

"He's been worried since the birth. He says that all he knows of Fire Drakes implies it should have been born breathing fire."

"Doesn't he have any information on it in books or something?" I asked.

"Nicholas, The Keeper was a Keeper of the world's myths long before he was The Zoo Keeper. He has kept myths in his head all his life so he could pass them down, generation after generation. A while back, the MBWF got really upset because more and more Mythical Beasts were perishing from habitat destruction, poaching, and just plain fear and superstition. So they begged The Keeper to take on the job at the Zoo. It wasn't long until he realized, if myths were to survive, he would have to educate humans. Hence, the tours and the resulting problems."

"How long ago did he become The Zoo Keeper?" Olivia asked.

"I don't know," Dr. Lang answered. "I'm afraid to ask. I think it's been a long, long, long time. "

"He's even older than he seems, huh?" I commented.

Dr. Lang shrugged.

"I didn't know you could live to be older than one hundred," Olivia said softly.

"One hundred?"

"That's how old I had decided The Keeper must be."

Dr. Lang shrugged and muttered, "I'd guess that was an underestimate, Olivia."

She led us through a tunnel-like passage-way built of rough stones that led into an absolutely spic and span, modern facility. The air was moist and smelled of something I couldn't place.

"It smells like babies," Olivia announced.

She was right. We were in the nursery. I wasn't much on babies since our little cousin Wilbur had been born. Every time I had held him, he had either wet on me or thrown up on me. Still, I had to admit these guys were pretty cute.

They were housed in various sized cubicles and glass, incubator type containers. A chart hung on each cubicle showing growth and food consumption, developmental accomplishments and physical characteristics.

"I'm trying to chart and record the information so there will be a record," Dr. Lang explained. "If someone had this information about Fire Drakes, I might be able to help ours."

"Dr. Lang, how come you work here?" I asked. "You seem like a normal person. Do you believe all this is real?"

"Think about it, Nicholas. If I do believe, this is the opportunity of a life time, and it's hard not to believe once you have delivered a Nyah-Gwaheh, and it's a breech birth, and you have to perform a Caesarean Section."

"What's all that mean?" O asked.

"A breech birth is when the baby is turned upside down when it needs to come out of the mother. If you don't make an incision in the mommy's tummy and take it out, the mother and the baby will die."

"What's a Nyah-Gwaheh?" I asked.

"That," said Dr. Lang, pointing to what looked like a bear cub.

"That's a bear," I said.

"True, but it will grow up to be bigger than the biggest Kodiak ever recorded and bigger by a lot. And, this little guy seems to magically make toys we give it vanish. The Iroquois say a Nyah-Gwaheh has lots of magical abilities."

I scratched my head and moved to another cubicle.

"What's this?" I asked, pointing to what looked like a blue-jay-sized bird with a dog's head and paws.

"Senmury, from Russia. Here," she said, reaching in and picking it up. She handed it to me. "You can hold it. It loves to be scratched behind the ears. It's three weeks old. Another week and it'll be back outside with the rest of the flock. It likes people a lot."

"What can I hold?" Olivia asked.

"If you're really careful, Olivia, you can hold our three-day-old Leontophontes. It's an orphan, so love it a lot."

Dr. Lang handed O an animal the size of a newborn kitten. It had a tail and mane of what looked like leaves from an Azalea bush.

"Oooh, it's so little and floppy," Olivia cried, cradling it against herself.

"You can feed it in a little while, Olivia."

"What does it eat?"

"Ants," Dr. Lang said, making Olivia squinch up her face.

"Mom wants some pictures. Do you mind taking a few of us with these guys, Dr. Lang?"

So, we hammed it up, and oohed and ahhed while Dr. Lang snapped photos.

"We have twelve mythical babies here and about thirty-five 'real' animals. All are endangered, both the 'real' and the mythical. Come over here kids," she said after we put the Senmury and Leontophontes back. "This is a young Bena from Malay," she said pointing to a large, water-filled tank in the corner. "It's an estuary dragon just sent to us by the MBWF. It can't fly or leave the water, but it can breath in both water and air and is a beautiful swimmer."

"It's so cute!" Olivia exclaimed as it did a few flips and turns. We watched it, fascinated until Dr. Lang called to us.

"Come here kids. This is really fun to watch. This is a Cactus Cat from the good, old U.S.A. It's mom and dad live in the desert habitat. It's had pneumonia, so it's been here a week."

She pulled on heavy gloves and shoved a large piece of prickly pear cactus through a trap door into the cubicle. The little, lynx-like cat sniffed at the cactus, pushing at it with a bony protrusion jutting from its front leg. Quickly it sliced the cactus open with the scythe like extension, scooped out the flesh of the plant and devoured it happily, sweetly purring.

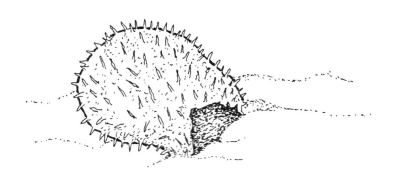

"Does it only eat cacti, I hope?" I asked.

"That's all," Dr. Lang confirmed. "I want you to see our two, latest acquisitions. One is from Ireland and one from Russia. I'm glad they're healthy because I would have absolutely no idea how to treat them if they weren't."

"Why not?" I asked.

"Because they are both shape shifters and I would have no idea which shape to treat," she told us.

"I can see that," I mumbled.

The Irish Pooka was nocturnal, so it was sleeping in its day shape, a curled up baby goat. Dr. Lang tried to rouse it and it vanished.

"Hey, where'd it go?" Olivia cried.

"It's still there. It has just become invisible. It's quite cute at one in the morning and very playful, but during the day it's hopelessly lethargic and every time I've tried to arouse it, it has vanished."

The Lesouik was much more concrete. It lacked the invisibility feature. When we first looked at it, it looked like a Labrador puppy, but in a split second, it turned into a Nine Banded

Armadillo. The floor was covered in layers of saw dust, but even though it romped around its cubicle, no matter where it tread, it never left tracks. Dr. Lang scooped it up. It nuzzled her cheek gently, rolled into a ball, shifted once again, this time into a Squirrel Monkey and crawled onto her shoulder.

"It's very gentle and doesn't allow harm to come to anyone or anything. Here Nick, hold it a minute."

As soon as she handed it to me it shifted into a Tarantula. I nearly dropped it, but Olivia caught it just as it shifted into an Elephant Shrew.

"Uh, here, Dr. Lang," Olivia said, quickly returning it to the veterinarian who was smiling broadly.

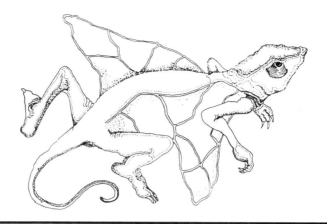

"Hey, cut it out," I yelled as something pulled on my shirt sleeve. At the sound of my voice a little, winged lizard backed off, eyes wide.

"I'm sorry," I whispered holding out my hand. It winged over to me and crawled onto my palm and up my shirt sleeve.

"That tickles," I giggled as quietly as possible.

"I'm surprised the Tazelwurm has taken to you like that Nick. It's very, very shy normally. It lives quite a solitary life in the mountains of Switzerland," Dr. Lang told us.

"I hope it doesn't want to live in my shirt," I said as it crawled out at the neck.

"Smile, Nicky," Olivia said, taking my picture just as the Tazelwurm tickled me again.

"Oh my, it's late," Dr. Lang said. "I've got an appointment with The Keeper and your father. Come on Nicholas, let's put the Tazelwurm back."

The trouble was, the Tazelwurm kept slithering out of our grasp and finding its way back up my shirt, making me gasp as its tail tickled my skin and it wriggled around on my back.

"Good grief," Dr. Lang commented. "At this rate, you may have to take it home with you."

"Maybe when it goes to sleep later, we can bring it back," I suggested.

"Nick, it doesn't sleep. Why don't you take your shirt off, but wait a minute." She came back with a net. "Now, Nicholas."

I whipped off my shirt over my head and she scooped the Tazlewurm up in the net and into a cage as swiftly as she could. It pressed its little feet and face up against the glass walls and stared at me plaintively.

"Poor thing," Olivia said. "Why don't you leave it your shirt, Nicky?"

"Olivia, it's my last clean shirt. Mom hasn't found a washing machine to do the laundry. They do it all by hand at the Zoo. So bye, bye little guy," I said to the Tazelwurm. "I'll be back."

We left, but not before Olivia took one last photo of the little lizard.

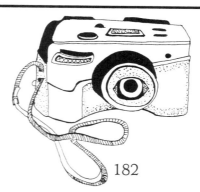

182

CHAPTER 16

When we got back to the main building, Dr. Lang rushed off to The Keeper's study. She was hoping he'd have time to look in on the Fire Drake. Olivia and I wandered about the court-yard discussing the nursery when I heard something.

"Shh, Olivia," I said trying to hear better. "Did you hear anything?"

She cocked her head, but it was silent. We sat at the table and dealt a hand of Old Maid with a dog-eared deck that spoke of Gargoylian ownership. The corners were tattered and the cards were crinkled, but most of all they smelled vaguely of Gargoyles. Again, I thought I heard something. Looking up, I saw a short-beaked, green parrot watching us. I tapped Olivia and pointed.

"Hi," Olivia whispered, hoping not to frighten it.

"Hi," the bird called back.

We smiled and looked at each other.

"I'm Olivia."

"Hi, Olivia," it said.

"I'm Nick."

"I'm Kendrick Kekeko from Indonesia."

Now we looked at each other without smiling.

"Kendrick, um, you can talk?"

"Sure. I speak English, Indonesian, Russian, Malay, Chinese, Farsi, Tamil and . . ."

"Okay, okay. You must be a mythical bird," I interrupted.

"Of course he is, Nicky," Olivia admonished as if I was being stupid.

"I am not, Miss Olivia. I am quite real, flesh and blood, in existence, quite alive."

"You sure do go on and on, Kendrick," Gideon said, floating down from his tower. "The Keeper thought you might show up with kids around. Kendrick can't resist kids. It's part of his nature," Gideon explained.

"True. I love children. They are delightful, darling, naughty but lovable, and increasingly rare at the Zoo."

"Look Kendrick, The Keeper wants to see

you. You've got some business to settle with him."

"I am not interested in further negotiations on the issue of curtailing my appearances or other activities, Gideon."

"Aw Kendrick, I've got no choice. I've got to bring you in. He made me promise," Gideon sighed.

"I doubt if you can catch me, Gideon, but in any case, I wouldn't try if I were you, unless you want The Keeper to know of your plans and plottings in regard to a certain issue."

Gideon stopped short in mid-air and whirled towards the pesky parrot.

"You nosy little so and so. Why don't you stay out of other creatures' affairs?"

"Not in my nature, Gideon. So, I'm leaving. Nice to meet you kids. Be seeing you around," he called as he sped off.

"Gideon!" I said turning, catching his eye. "What plot?"

"Nicholas, you can't think anything of what that vociferous, little snoop says."

"Gideon!"

"Forget it, Nick, no way," he yelled as he too sped off.

"Nicky, what's going on?" O asked.

"Who knows? They're both crazy."

"Yes, but Nicky, they are not special effects."

"No, I don't think so," I agreed.

We went back to our card game until Dad came rambling by.

"Hey, kids. I haven't had time to see much of you in days. What have you been up to?"

"We got to spend the afternoon in the nursery. A Tazelwurm tried to adopt Nicky. Daddy can we take it home when we go?"

Dad rubbed his eyes wearily. "What's a Tazelwurm?"

"Guess, Daddy."

"I'm sorry, Olivia. I'm too tired to guess. Come on. Let's go upstairs and see Mom," he said, putting an arm around each of us.

"Dad, do you have any idea what the Gargoyles are up to?" I asked.

"I doubt if anyone can keep track of the Gargoyles."

"Yes, but Dad, I think they are going to do something they shouldn't again."

"Listen Nick, I'm sure they've done that so many times it would be abnormal for them to behave. Come on, Mom and I want to tell you guys about all the plans we've been making for the Zoo. Everything is moving right along. It has to, because I don't have much leave left."

"Dad, I'm glad you picked this trip, and I'm glad you decided to help the Zoo. It's a great place, isn't it O?"

"I love it here, Daddy. It's the best summer you ever planned."

"I agree, Dad, but it's also the only good summer you have ever planned."

"You may be right, Nick. I'm glad I finally got one right," he said without argument.

We found Mom in our room, sitting on the floor in the middle of piles of papers.

"These are the letters we've prepared to invite schools to participate in our program," she explained, trying to gather them into neat piles.

While Dad showered, Olivia and I got out a game of Marvin's Maze to play. Clearing a spot on the floor among the papers, we had just begun when Dad came back and flopped onto a bed. He looked tired, but more relaxed. For once his hair wasn't combed perfectly and he had even left a couple of buttons on his shirt undone.

Olivia noticed too because she whispered, "Nicky, you can see Dad's undershirt and it's not even white."

She was right. It was pale yellow, a major deviation from Dad's personal conventions.

"Martha, why don't you tell the kids what you've been doing."

"Well, I've prepared these letters inviting schools to participate in an educational field trip to the Mt. Olympus Zoo. For a nominal fee, the day long tour will take classes through special environments containing exhibits of various species of mythical beasts. Knowledgeable keepers will accompany each group, giving background and answering questions. At the end of the tour, each child and teacher will receive an educational packet, including *The Deluxe Mt. Olympus Zoo Bestiary* for their school library. Now then, what do you two think ?"

"Sounds great, Mom. I didn't know you could write stuff like that," I said.

She threw a pair of my clean socks at me, which I caught.

"At last, you did the laundry. Thanks, Mom. I was worried I was going to have to wear these pants for a fourth day."

"Actually, I didn't have time, so The Keeper had Grant and George do it. They complained and complained, but I think they did a good job."

"I guess so, Mom, but I think they put in a little too much starch," I said, holding up stiffened socks.

"Whoops," Mom said.

Ignoring the laundry issue, Dad asked, "How soon do you think we can get our information out so we can give our presentation, Martha?"

"The letters are going out tomorrow. The Gargoyles are going to stamp them tonight and The Keeper will send someone to the post office tomorrow to mail them."

"I had a brief image of grey, Gargoylian

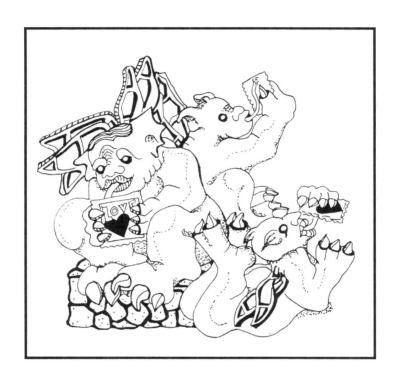

tongues licking love stamps and pressing them onto envelopes, their eyes glowing under the light of the moon.

"As for the brochures and the first bestiaries, they should be ready in about two more days. The Keeper has four of the younger keepers running an old hand press they have in a cellar. As the books come off the press, an elderly Gargoyle is illuminating them in gold leaf. They are truly gorgeous, a memorable and to be treasured souvenir, but it's slow work. Why, Harold?"

"Because, I've invited the Zoning Commissioners for a tour in four more days and I want to be sure everything will be ready. I thought Nicholas might want to act as a Junior Tour Guide. The Keeper and I are a little nervous about the Gargoyles being too available. Our next biggest worry is whether or not we can impress the Commissioners enough to win them over and get our official permit."

"Is there any word on a law suit?" I asked.

"Nope. It looks like we got reliable information on that. Thanks, Nick."

"Think nothing of it. The experience made

me consider being a spy when I grew up, until the reprimand, at least."

"Really?" a new voice asked from the window.

"Kendrick!" Olivia and I shouted.

"Of course, who'd you expect?" the bird asked.

"Actually, we weren't expecting anyone," Dad answered.

"By the way, Mr. Powers, your plan sounds sound, well thought out, convincing and substantial," Kendrick offered.

"Kendrick, you snoop," Gideon yelled, flying in through the door.

"Whoops, got to fly," Kendrick shouted. "Bye, now."

"That bird!" Gideon complained, doing a belly flop onto my bed. "I've been chasing him all day, but he's slippery. So, I've decided to stick to you kids like a shadow until he reappears."

"Get off my bed, Gideon!" I shouted. "You can't stay here unless you get cleaned up."

"Cleaned?" Gideon looked at Dad. "Do I

really, really have to, Mr. Powers? It's not my fault that hanging around here is the only way I can think of to catch Kendrick."

"If you want to stick around us, you'll have to bathe. Nick and Olivia will help scrub you," Dad said, confirming my ultimatum.

"Bathe? Yuck," Gideon groaned. "Truly?"

We all nodded our heads in unison.

"Oh woe, oh woe. The Keeper has threatened to take away my midnight snacks if I can't catch Kendrick, and this seems to be the only way. Woe, woe," he moaned as we marched off to the bathroom.

Filling the tub with hot water, and equipped with long handled, bristle brushes and scouring cleanser, we began to scrub the squat, little Gargoyle. We had to refill the tub three times before the water stayed clear enough to rinse him. He muttered and mumbled and bemoaned his fate the whole while. Finally we toweled him off and marched him back to the room.

"Is that you, Gideon?" Grant asked from where he was perched on the hearth.

"Who do you think it is?" Gideon snarled.

"What happened to you?" Grant asked, open mouthed.

"I did it for love of duty and to catch Kendrick," Gideon spat.

Grant looked at George who had just waddled through the door.

"That's what we came to tell you," George whispered. "Kendrick turned himself in. He said he didn't want to get you into any more trouble."

"What!" Gideon exploded. "I took a bath to catch him and that stupid bird walked up to The Keeper all by himself."

"You look great, Gideon," Mom tried to console him.

"And you smell great," I added.

"All sweet and soapy," Olivia said.

"Sure, sure, you would think that," he yelled in our faces and flew out the door.

George and Grant looked embarrassed as they excused themselves politely.

CHAPTER 17

The day of the tour grew closer. The Keeper decided a less dramatic guide than himself was in order for the occasion and picked the young Keeper Robert. Gideon had magically vanished from sight and Grant was making himself scarce as well. I figured Gideon was sulking about his embarrassing, newly imposed cleanliness, but in the back of my mind, I remembered Kendrick's accusations and the peculiar congregation of Gargoyles in the courtyard that Grant had carefully avoided talking about. The night before the big day, I decided to see if I could find Gideon. I wandered into the courtyard and peered up into the turrets above the gate, but no Gargoyles were visible from that angle, although two, gleaming spots stared eerily back at me. I scanned the walls and the sky, but there were no Gargoyles perching anywhere, nor winging about the darkened sky. I jumped as something rubbed against my leg. Looking down, I found a large house cat rubbing up against me and reached down to pat it. It looked up at me with piercing eyes that glowed brightly in the dark, lighting up its whole face. It

stared at me fixedly, without flinching, in a distractingly intelligent way.

"It's a Ccoa. Be careful of offending it," a Gargoyle I had never seen offered.

"Why?"

"It's rather autocratic and doesn't take lightly to disrespect," the Gargoyle said. "I suppose you are Gideon's infamous human-boy, Nicholas? I'm Gamial."

"Are you the Gamial who knows all the Gargoylian myths?"

"I am. I am the Official Mythologist of Gargoylian culture, it's true, but, at the moment I am in search of Gideon or Grant or George or Gerald or Gimmy or Guinivere or Ginny or any of the younger Gargoyles. Have you seen any of them?"

"You are the first Gargoyle I've seen in two or three days. I thought Gideon was off sulking because we gave him the scrubbing of his life."

"Ah yes, he is so clean, the pores of his stone are visible, poor little fellow. Perhaps it does explain Gideon's absence, but what about the rest of them?"

"You've got me, but I'll bet Kendrick Kekeko knows," I said.

"Maybe, but he flew the coop two days ago himself and no one has seen him either. It makes me uneasy."

"Somebody better warn The Keeper," I said.

"Of what? We know nothing, really. I hate to bother him when he's so worried about the baby Fire Drake, who is worsening at a faster and faster rate. And The Keeper has, after all, asked us to restrain ourselves from appearances during the visit tomorrow. Perhaps that is all that is happening," Gamial pointed out.

I wasn't convinced and I didn't think he was either.

"Well, Nicholas, let me know if you find them," Gamial said. He flapped up to where I had seen the two glittering spots and called out, "There's a Hercinia up here."

"What's that?" I yelled back.

"Only a bird about the size of a jay, but its eyes glow at night in a very disconcerting fashion," Gamial told me as he settled into a Gargoylian crouch.

"Thanks," I called, noticing the Ccoa had slipped off.

I went into the kitchen for a snack. It too was oddly empty of Gargoyles. They were usually raiding the refrigerator all night. Grant was particularly fond of the cook's home-made ice cream, but the entire batch in the freezer was untouched. I shook my head and decided against eating. Instead, I went back to our room. The lights were out and everyone was sleeping.

"Olivia, do you know where Gideon is?" I asked, trying to awaken her without awakening Mom and Dad. She buried herself deeper under the covers. I pulled at them and shook her a little.

"Go away, Nicky," she mumbled.

"Come on, Olivia."

"He said something about a quest, something about heroic and dangerous deeds to save the baby Fire Drake. You know the little guy is getting worse. He coughs all the time now," she mumbled.

"Olivia, try and think," I insisted.

She opened her eyes a little more.

"Nicky, I don't know anything else, except Dr. Lang thinks that if the baby Fire Drake doesn't breathe fire within two or three days, he's going to die. The Gargoyles are really upset."

"I didn't know it was that serious."

"Well, it is," she said sadly. "Oh, Nicky, I don't want him to die."

"Me either. Go back to sleep, O. It's going to be okay, I know it."

I helped her pull the covers up, went to the window and looked out. It was disconcerting to see Gamial keeping his singular vigil. Usually this late at night the parapets along the wall were lined with Gargoyles. I put my shoes back on and sneaked out and down to the courtyard again.

"Gamial, I don't think they're coming back

tonight," I called. "My sister, Olivia, just told me Gideon mentioned going on a quest and performing heroic deeds to save the baby Fire Drake."

Gamial flapped down to where I stood.

"Heroic deeds indeed. Humph. These young, Gargoylian whipper-snappers couldn't save their own pock-marked hides, much less a baby Fire Drake. They don't even know the meaning of the words, 'heroic deeds.' There hasn't been a truly heroic deed since the days of Gabriel Garfeld Garrard Gargoyle the Great, the four G Gargoyle of all times.

"It was back in the summer of 1897 human time, when I first saw him fly into these hills. He was the biggest Gargoyle I have ever met. His head was heavy and he wore a dark patch over one eye. He wore a short vest of chain mail as if it weighed nothing. He had seen many a battle in his day."

The rhythm of Gamial's deep, throaty voice entranced me.

"In those days, humans had not yet come into our mountains. They were only mythical creatures with which to scare young Gargoyles.

Our perches were near rich veins of stone and we roamed across vast outcroppings of rock without trepidation, but slowly, the stories of humans began to spread and our fears began to magnify themselves. We stopped roaming without going in groups and we felt as if we were constantly looking over our wings to see if the humans were there, until the day Gabriel the Great flapped into camp. He rambled among us, and listened to our tales, and heard our fears under the midnight stars. Finally, one moonless night, his voice silenced us as he rumbled, 'Gargoyles of the Rock,' for this was how we were known then. 'Gargoyles of the Rock, I have seen the human monsters and they are nothing to fear. It is true, they are soft to the touch. And, it is true, they roam in the day while we are asleep and vulnerable. But, they are also easily scared and unimaginative. Their weapons are only useful against soft creatures like themselves and they are afraid of the dark.'

"All the Gargoyles of the Rock were silent, which was unheard of in a gathering of Gargoyles. It was easy to see our terror at the thought of our worst fears being confirmed. The humans were real. Across our minds ran all the stories of how humans terrorized and stalked

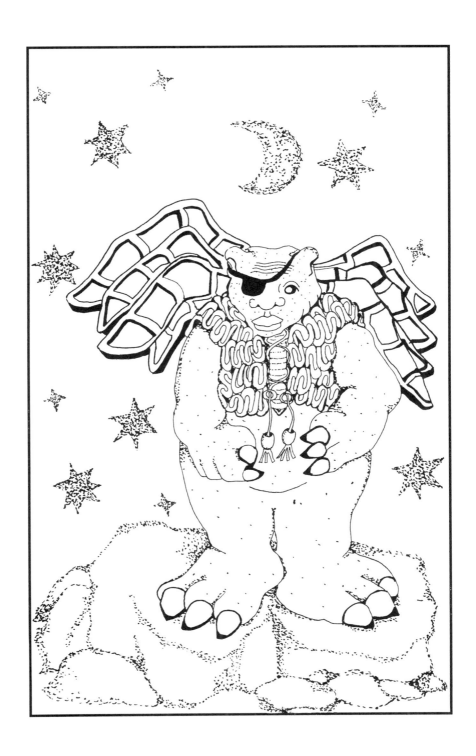

Gargoyles, imprisoning them in cages and tormenting them until they turned forever to stone. We stood frozen in terror.

"Gabriel saw what he had done to us and raising his deep voice said, 'Do not worry. I will capture a human and bring it to you and you will see, they are nothing to fear.'

"No one said anything as he flew off alone that night. Many days passed and he did not return. We grew more and more uneasy and not a few felt guilty for letting him go alone, but no one dared to look for him. The days stretched out until, just before dawn as we all grew sleepy, a week before my seventeenth birthday, Gabriel flew heavily into camp. He carried a human in his arms, probably no more than ten of your years. The boy was sobbing in terror as Gabriel set him down.

"No one touched him. We were afraid. I could not imagine how Gabriel had had the courage to carry him cradled in his arms for so long.

"Gabriel broke the spell saying, 'I searched many days until I found this human who could be easily borrowed without alerting the other humans. His kind stay far from here and usually stay together. They speak of legends of monsters in the hills and build fires to light their nights and keep the monsters at bay. I spent many nights perched above their campfires listening to their tales, before this one wandered off. They are as fearful and full of superstitions about us as we are about them.

"'When you have satisfied your curiosity about humans, I will return this one to his home. Do not harm him or taunt him, or be unkind, for he is very frightened. But, at least you can see you need not be afraid of a creature like this.'

"And indeed we weren't, and almost forgot about the humans, for they were no longer myths or something to be feared, but Gabriel was wrong as it turned out," Gamiel sighed. "We should have been wary and frightened, for the human's greatest weapon was neither an axe nor a spear nor a gun, but their ability to multiply quickly and their voracious consumption of the land for their own needs."

Gamiel finished and sighed again, shaking his head sadly.

Finally I said, "I'm sorry."

"Yes, you probably are. In any case, these young Gargoyles are fools. Quests in groups of twenty, what nonsense! There's hardly any risk in that. Not one of them has one tenth the courage of Gabriel. All combined, they don't have his courage."

"Twenty? That's a lot of missing Gargoyles," I commented. "I wonder what they are really up to?"

"Let's hope it is not stealing humans," Gamial answered.

"Oh, my! You didn't just tell them this story recently did you? I mean, they seem to get all kinds of impulsive ideas from things they hear or read," I explained.

"I've noticed that as well, but it's quite safe. I haven't mentioned this particular tale in many years."

"Thank goodness. I could just imagine them kidnapping some famous veterinarian or someone," I sighed in relief.

"You look tired young Nicholas. Go to bed. Quit worrying. They'll be back," Gamial comforted me as he returned to his perch on the wall.

I was dead tired by the time I got to bed, but I never slept very well. I kept wondering what those inept Gargoyles were up to.

CHAPTER 18

The morning was an uproar of preparations and last minute instructions. Dad was to be the official representative of the Zoo. Dressed in the only good clothes he had brought, a wolf-print tie and a sports coat, he looked moderately professional until the baby Tazelwurm got loose out of my arms and couldn't be coached or pried off his shoulder.

Dr. Lang and The Keeper were trying to think of a solution when the first members of the

Zoning Commission were spotted outside the gate. At the last minute, I raced upstairs, into our room and tore through the dirty laundry until I found the shirt I had worn the day the Tazelwurm had crawled down my back. I ran back to Dad and waved it in front of the little lizard until, just as the first of the Commissioners knocked at the Great Gate, it jumped into the shirt.

One of the Keepers ushered the group in as I cradled the T-shirt-wrapped Tazelwurm against my chest. Every once in a while, as my dad gave a decorous and elegant greeting to another Commissioner, the Tazelwurm made me smile as it wriggled against my ribs.

"Welcome, Ladies and Gentlemen. Let me offer you this brochure about our institution. I'm sure you'll be impressed with the Zoo," Dad said, handing out the beautifully gold-leafed pamphlets.

"This is very impressive, Mr. Powers. I'll be interested, as I'm sure we all will be, to see which Mythical Beasts are represented in your zoo. I, myself, am particularly interested in the Desert Realm you mention here. I've always loved the desert," a tall, athletic looking man said.

"Well then, why don't we start there. Our guide today will be Keeper Robert. He'll be able to give you an excellent tour," Dad said suavely.

"Delightful," an elderly woman said. "And who are you young man?" she asked me.

"Nicholas Powers, Ma'am," I said politely.

"And why are you holding a wadded-up tee shirt, Nicholas?"

I looked nervously at Dad who thought a second and nodded.

"Uh, I've got a Tazelwurm in here. It originates in Switzerland. Its normal habitat is mountainous," I answered truthfully.

"Can I see it?" she asked with a quizzical smile.

"Sure," I said, unwrapping it, but being sure to keep the lizard in a tight grasp. "What's unusual about the Tazelwurm is that it can fly," I explained.

"Oh my, it's darling. How clever to present it as a baby," another lady said. "Look how real it is!"

I smiled as it wriggled in my hands and managed to slide under my shirt.

"Now that is a clever trick, young man. Very well done," another Commissioner said.

"Now, if you will follow me," Keeper Robert announced.

We followed a trail of sand as the Commissioners commented to each other about this or that. I was too busy trying to control the Tazelwurm to pay much attention.

"Ladies and Gentlemen, we have come to the Desert Realm of the Mt. Olympus Zoo," Robert announced in a beautiful baritone and his best tour-guide guise. "There are a few rules. Please do not touch or feed the animals. You will see things that we hope will both amaze you and make you wonder."

The Commissioners looked a bit embarrassed by Robert's sincerity until my Dad stepped in.

"As you can see, Ladies and Gentlemen, we intend to present our information in the most imaginative, informative and accurate way possible. After all, our aim is for The Zoo to offer an exciting and fun way to learn."

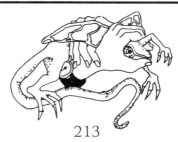

"Is it fun, young man?" someone asked me.

"Oh, yes! This has been the best. My sister and I have learned gobs. And, not just about Greek and Roman mythology like we do in school. We've learned about South American and North American native myths, Swiss, like this guy," I said pointing to the Tazelwurm, "Baltic, Medieval European, Egyptian, Persian, Indian." I went on and on, feeling a little like Kendrick.

"The list is as extensive as we can make it," Robert said, stopping me. "As you can imagine, many of the animals in a desert are not always obvious and may be well camouflaged. If you spot something interesting, feel free to ask questions. In a moment we will come to a large, glass-sided hill. The glass is tinted so that we don't disturb the inhabitants. The Mermax originate in Europe, although a similar creature exists in India. They have many characteristics of the common ant, but as you will see, are much larger."

We arrived at the wall. The ants were the size of mice. Some bore tusks. All were busily rushing about. In one corner of the hill were piles of something shiny. The Mermax walked about

totally unaware of us. After several minutes of fascinated staring, Robert continued.

"The tusked ants are the soldiers, the others the workers. Basically harmless, they seek both food and gold in their daily excursions out of the colony. If either gold or food is found, they leave a chemical trail behind them to lead other ants back to the find."

He stopped and we all watched for several minutes before a lady commented, "You are right. This is highly convincing. The ants are extremely realistic, as are their tunnels."

"Confound it, Ethel, how would you know?" a man asked.

"As it happens, I was trained as an ento-mologist," she answered.

Dad hurried us on. Maintaining ambiguity was one of his goals. Cacti bloomed along the path in a beautiful array. A full grown Cactus Cat darted out, sliced off a large chunk of cactus and ran off.

The Commissioners pointed and shouted as Robert calmly said, "Felis cactus, related to Felis lynx, native of North American deserts."

Someone commented to Dad, "The guide is quite good. He makes it so convincing."

"Thank you, we try," Dad smiled.

"We don't even have to try too hard, do we Tazelwurm?" I whispered to the little, winged lizard, as I stroked his head.

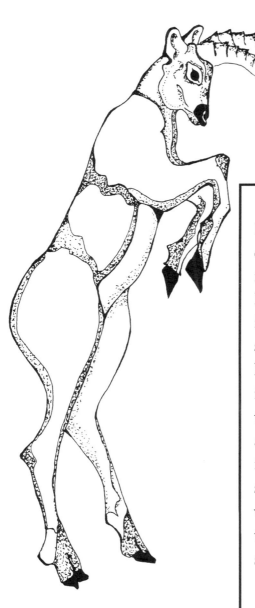

"Look up, Nicholas," Robert called just in time for me to see a large ram, standing statuesquely still with its two horns pointing forward. Its head turned towards us and the next instant it was a streak of motion, vanishing behind the curve of a sand dune.

"That is an Arabian Qata, reputed to be one

of the fastest animals on earth, for obvious reasons," Robert said.

"Or an extremely fast, motorized, remote controled contraption," a man remarked. I smiled, remembering our own skepticism when we first arrived.

"I'll say," another agreed. "Mr. Powers, this is great stuff."

"I'm glad you're enjoying it," Dad said.

"What's next? I can hardly wait," someone said.

"Watch the sand next to the paths for two species of snakes," Robert suggested. "One is Cerastes, a small snake of Egyptian origin. It carries two, horny protrusions above its eyes, which, after burying itself, it leaves sticking out of the sand to attract birds and small rodents. It is harmless to man. In fact, it is reputed to detect poisons and ward off the evil eye."

"The evil eye. Gee, I could use that at school when I get in trouble with my teachers," I

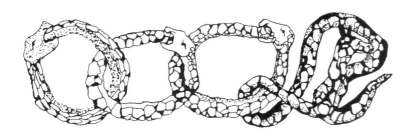

proclaimed, making Dad clear his throat and give me an evil eye, while everyone else laughed.

"The other is a Hoop Snake. This is one of our more common snakes, sighted frequently throughout the world. It moves rapidly by tucking its tail into its mouth and rolling like a hoop."

We all wandered along, our heads bent looking for the snakes, but all we spotted were some fairly large, black spiders.

"Are those some of your mythical beasts?" the entomologist lady inquired curiously.

"Actually, not these," Robert answered. "But, spiders are part of the larger mythological picture. The spider is frequently a weaver of fate. In some societies, a spider weaves illusion while in others the spider is considered to be lucky. The spider is found world wide, but we do not have any of the unusual, mythical species yet, although we hope to acquire some soon."

A shadow passed overhead and I looked up expecting to see one of the great birds, but instead it was a lone Gargoyle.

"My, what is that?" one of the ladies pointed.

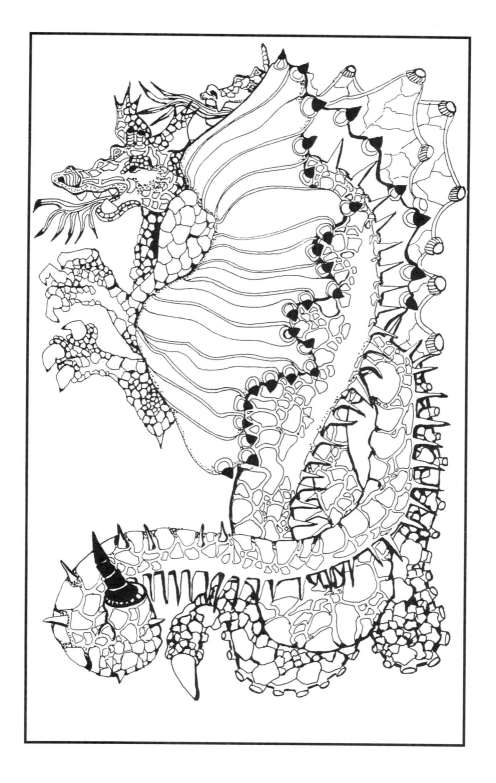

"A Gargoyle, madam," Robert said, shading his eyes with an odd expression on his face.

"I believe it's a flock of Gargoyles," Dad stammered.

"And me," shouted one Kekeko as he landed on my shoulder.

"And what's that behind them?" a man shouted.

It was hard to tell with the sun in our eyes, but it was certain that two large forms were hot on the Gargoyles' tails.

"Kendrick," I said in a hushed voice, "what is going on? What are those things?"

"A pair of adult Fire Drakes," he whispered back.

"What?" I gulped.

Before I could warn Dad, the Fire Drakes roared out flames at the Gargoyles. Dad nearly turned as blue as The Keeper's finger nails and even Robert gasped, but one of the men yelled, "This is terrific. What a show!"

"Show?" Kendrick asked. "You mean performance, act, entertainment?" he continued, flying right up to the man's face, who looked slightly perturbed by Kendrick's proximity.

The entomologist suddenly asked, "What is going on up there?"

Dad and Robert were at a complete loss, so I took a wild guess.

"The Gargoyles have lured the adult Fire Drakes here by," and I stopped not knowing how they had done it.

"Stealing the gold the Fire Drakes guard," Kendrick said, taking over quickly.

"Yeah, thanks Kendrick. That's it. They did it to save a baby Fire Drake that was hatched here a short time ago and is dying."

"Fire Drakes are highly endangered," Robert picked up as calmly as possible.

"Only," Kendrick added, "the Gargoyles didn't count on the Fire Drakes being quite so upset. Do you think Dr. Lang will be prepared?"

"Probably not," Dad said. "Nick, could you go tell her what's coming?" he added, a bit nervously.

"This is terrific. What a script," a man said.

That was all I heard, except for Robert trying to continue as if it was exactly that, a script. As soon as I was out of sight I ran, Kendrick fluttering along beside me, the Tazelwurm digging his claws into my skin and holding on for dear life.

"Go Kendrick, go. Warn The Keeper. I'll go to Dr. Lang."

I looked up behind me. The Gargoyles were circling in what I hoped was delaying tactics, but looked more like confusion. I wondered if stone could be scorched by Dragon's breath? If so, there were going to be some scarred Gargoyles. I was drinking in gasps of hot air that seemed a bit smoky as I ran, and my legs were getting heavier and heavier. It seemed like forever before I saw the nursery.

"Dr. Lang," I screamed, but only Olivia came out.

"Quiet Nicky, the babies are sleeping," she said in what seemed like an inane comment at the moment.

"Out of my way, O. The Fire Drakes are coming. Those crazy Gargoyles brought them to save the baby. I'm going to wring that Gideon's neck."

Olivia looked up and her mouth dropped. She ran inside for Dr. Lang as I headed for the baby Fire Drake's cell.

"Nicholas, what's going on?" Dr. Lang pleaded as she appeared.

I just pointed as gold coins started raining from the Gargoyles as they passed overhead. Apparently, they were trying to drop them into the baby's cage, but they were landing wildly, everywhere.

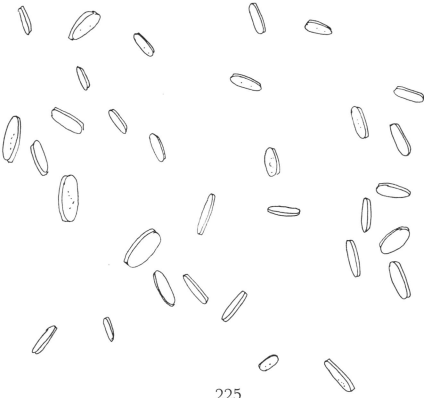

"Great Caesar's Ghost," Dr. Lang whispered hoarsely.

"You said it. Let's take cover," I yelled.

The Gargoyles were veering away, but the Fire Drakes were heading straight for the nursery and their stolen gold.

"We can't leave the baby," Olivia shouted.

"Oh, yes you can," The Keeper said as he ran up. "Inside, now."

"But . . ."

"Now," he yelled, as the two adult dragons landed all too close. One of them peered easily over the twelve foot high walls of the baby's cubicle and sniffed at it. The other was suddenly blocking our path and we were trapped.

"Don't move, don't twitch, don't say a thing," The Keeper breathed softly.

The Fire Drakes turned back to the baby. I held my breath, praying they wouldn't hurt it. They were too big to fit in the cubicle. One scrapped all the gold it could find into a pile and started scooping it into its mouth. The other kept peering at the baby. It was clear it wanted the rest of the gold that had randomly fallen into the

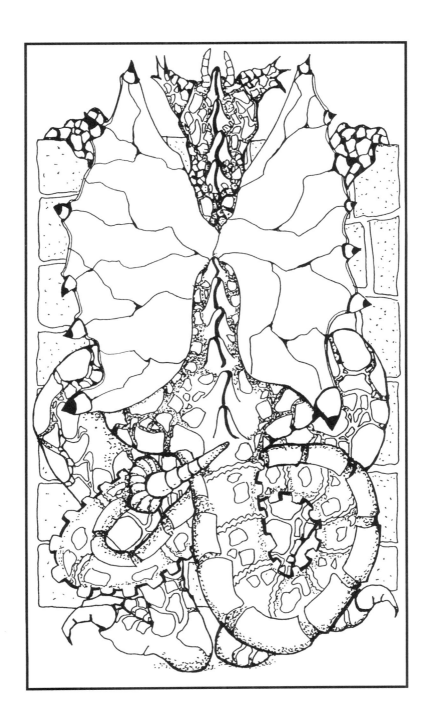

cubicle. The baby reared up onto its hind legs, wings spread, pitiful wisps of smoke issuing from its mouth. The Fire Drake nearest it sent out a whiff of flame straight at the baby, who coughed and flapped its wings, but couldn't fly yet.

Olivia whimpered. I risked a look at her. Tears were streaming down her face.

"Please, oh please, don't kill it," she said over and over under her breath.

Please don't kill us, I thought.

The baby coughed again and again, sinking to the ground, gagging horribly. With effort it raised its head, gasped again and hacked out a long wraith-like trail of fire at the bigger dragon. The adult dragons stepped back, as the baby began scrabbling at its gold, like a puppy digging a hole. Spitting fire all the while, he kicked out a rain of gold pieces onto the two adults who gulped them down like a couple of porpoises catching fish in mid-air. After a few minutes they roared again, spewing fire against one of the walls of the cage, scorching it black, and then raised their huge, red-veined wings and fled into the sky.

"I'll be," Dr. Lang expelled. "I guess the

baby could tell their gold from his."

"I'll spank the living daylights out of that Gideon," The Keeper gasped.

"No, I will," Gamial said, appearing from around the corner. "That idiot."

"Shall we share the pleasure then?" The Keeper inquired. "He has gone too far, much, much too far."

"But he cured the baby Fire Drake. It can breathe fire," Olivia pointed out.

Dr. Lang nodded as she looked at the little Dragon now sleeping on its pile of gold.

"Yes, and now what do we do with it?" The Keeper asked. "If those adults ever encounter it in the wild, they'll kill it. And it's already growing too big for its cage, but it will never leave its gold or allow us to transport it to some other spot."

"Let Gideon solve it," I suggested.

The Keeper and Gamial smiled simultaneously at my suggestion and were still smiling wickedly when Kendrick reappeared warning loudly, "Tourist alert! Commissioners headed this way. Tourist alert!"

The Keeper and Gamial vanished around the corner, arm in wing, smiles still on their faces. I didn't envy Gideon. Dad appeared with a tentative expression on his face.

"The Commissioners would like to see the baby Fire Drake. Is it all right?" he asked hesitantly, his eyes searching the area quickly.

"Sure," Dr. Lang smiled, pointing, "but be careful."

The Commissioners crowded around and the entomologist said, "Gee, this wall is hot."

"Well, the Fire Drakes were here," I said honestly, banking on the Commissioners' disbelief to protect us.

"You folks sure do put on a show. I can't imagine anyone not loving this place," a lady Commissioner said.

"Mr. Powers, unless someone comes up with a real good reason or concrete objection, we will be approving your application. It's been a real pleasure and I hope to visit here again soon," the Chairman of the Commission said.

They all shook Dad's hand and thanked Robert as they wandered back to the front gates. As soon as they were gone, we crowded into the courtyard, shouting congratulations and slapping each other on the back. The Keeper stood to one side smiling and nodding. Kendrick Kekeko buzzed about kibitzing and remarking verbosely on everything. Only Gideon and the Gargoylian-Fire-Drake-Brigade were absent.

"Gideon should be here," Olivia said.

"He could have ruined everything."

"I know, Nicky, but he should be here."

"He almost got us killed, O."

"I know," she said.

"But you miss him. I do too, but I bet he'll be here soon. He's incorrigible."

"Nicky, is the Tazelwurm still under your shirt?"

"Oh, my gosh, he is," I said.

"Well," said The Keeper from behind us, "I guess you may have to take him with you and raise him for us. Could you do that?"

"Really? Of course we could! Oh boy, oh boy," I yelled.

"But there is one condition. You and Olivia will have to bring him back next summer, when he's full grown, for us to see."

"It's a deal, if my dad and mom say its okay."

"I think they will, Nicholas. Your dad just agreed to be on retainer for the Zoo."

"That's terrific. Olivia, we can come back whenever we want to."

She threw her arms around me and kissed me right in public and said, "You know what I'm going to be when I grow up, Nicky? I'm going to be a mythologist just like Gamial."

"Not me. I'm going to be the guy who goes out and collects all the mythical animals for the Mt. Olympus Zoo," I proclaimed.

"And me, I'm going to be a lot more cautious," said Gideon as he landed gingerly on The Keeper's shoulder.

"I hope so," The Keeper said sternly.

"Gideon," O said. "I hope so too, because I missed you and if you're bad, you might not be here when we come back."

"Hey kid, don't get all mushy on me," Gideon said sheepishly.

"Don't worry about it, Gideon. She'll grow out of it, come to her senses and see you for what you are," I admonished.

Gideon stuck his tongue out at me.

CHAPTER 19

The next morning was dreary. There was a light, grey rain falling. The phone rang all morning with people wanting information and dates for trips to the Zoo. The Keeper decided he was going to need a secretary and more phone lines.

"I don't want to leave," I sulked.

"I know, Nick, but my leave is up," Dad said gently.

"But, you hate your job. Why don't we just stay here?"

"Nick," Mom said, hugging me, "we'll be back, and Gideon and Kendrick will correspond with us."

"Mommy," O said. "I love this place. Please, please, let us live here."

"Olivia," Dad said. "It's okay to visit here all we want, but unfortunately we have to live in the real world."

"You mean the human world," Gideon quipped from atop the gate.

"Yes, Gideon, that is exactly what I mean.

"But Dad," I asked, "you do believe, don't you?"

"Well, ah, well, Nick . . ."

"Oh, come on Harold, admit it. You believe. You've been wondering what it'll cost us to raise the Tazelwurm for heavens sake. He believes kids," Mom told us with a big grin.

Dad smiled and shrugged. It was as much as we could get out of him.

"Hey Olivia, how about a hug?" Gideon said bashfully as we got ready to go to the car. He glided down and stood in her path. She threw her arms around him.

"Oh, Gideon, you are starting to smell Gargoylian again."

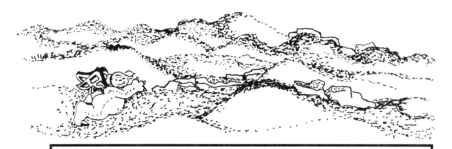

"Thank the many gods. And you will never, ever trick me into a bath like that again," he exclaimed as he stuck out his stony head for a kiss.

"Want to make a bet?" I asked.

"Sure. I'll bet you one hundred, honeyed rocks that next summer you don't get me within one hundred feet of a bath."

"It's a bet rock-head," I said.

"Okay, be good Kid," Gideon called as we piled into our car. He flew alongside us for a while and then wheeled off towards a rocky ridge.

The Tazelwurm nuzzled my ear. Olivia waved and I realized she was still trailing golden streaks from her fingers.

"Hey Dad, we're going to have to come up with a good explanation for Olivia's golden touch," I pointed out.

"You're right son. Got any suggestions?" he asked.

"Magic?" I asked.

He shook his head. "No one would believe that. How about saying she was in a lightning storm and her Kirlian Aura became visibly ionized?"

"Hey, that's perfect Dad. I didn't think you had it in you."

He smiled happily.

We came down off the mountain and back onto the highway. Cars barreled along at seventy-five miles an hour, filling our ears with their motors and their horns. The Tazelwurm dived under the front seat, barely peeking out. A truck honked loudly at us and the Tazelwurm backed the rest of the way under the seat.

"Can you get it out?" Dad asked. "I don't think it's safe for it to be loose in the car."

"I'll try, Dad, but I think you should pull into the next rest stop." That proved to be forty miles down the road and by then everyone needed to stop.

"Dad, will you get me a hamburger and a shake and I'll try and coax it out."

I was bent over, half in and half out of the

car when a kid came up and said, "Watcha doing?" He was about five, with a wide ring of chocolate ice cream around his mouth and a dripping cone clutched in his hand.

"Trying to get a friend of mine out from under the seat."

"What kind of friend?"

"A Tazelwurm," I muttered without thinking.

"Can I see what a Tazelwurm is?" he asked squirming into the car by stepping all over me.

The minute he was in, the Tazelwurm streaked out and buried its little face in the chocolate.

"Hey," the kid said, as I grabbed the Tazelwurm. "That thing ruined my ice cream!"

"Sorry," I called as the kid ran off, leaving me with a chocolate-covered Tazelwurm.

"What happened?" Olivia asked.

I just shook my head in disgust.

We got in the car and started back down the road as I tried to clean up my charge with some water from a thermos.

We hadn't gone too far when Mom said, "Maybe we'll be lucky and it'll go to sleep in the car like babies do."

"Ah, Mom, Dad, there is something about the Tazelwurm you might want to know."

"What's that?"

"He never sleeps."

"What?" they exclaimed together.

"Sorry," I said, but they didn't answer. "Well," I said. "It's better than bringing home a Gargoyle."

"Amen," they said together. "Amen."

MYTHOLOGICAL REFERENCES

Compiled and written by John Kenney

Aitvaras: This creature of Lithuanian legend is a composite of a cock and a dragon. When it flies at night, its tail resembles a spurt of fire. It lives in a farmhouse and demands omelets from the family with whom it is living. In return, it gives the household corn and coins, which it steals from neighboring farm houses.

Arctic Mole: Of Chinese origin, this beast is a large, walrus-like creature that has certain attributes of a mole, in that it burrows out tunnels, but under ice not soil. It is nocturnal, as any contact with sunlight causes its instant death.

Assyrian Winged Bull: This protective spirit guarded the gates to temples in Ancient Assyria, now part of Iraq. It took the form of a winged bull with a human face, usually the face of the king.

Bena: This is a Malaysian estuary dragon. It i is an outstanding swimmer, but cannot leave the water, even though it can breathe in ai as well as under water.

Bird Bear: This Icelandic bear-beast of huge bulk has an ineffectual set of wings.

Bird of Paradise: This bird, whose existence was reported by travellers to the east, was the size of a goose and had brilliant plumage, but had neither wings nor feet. It suspended itself from trees by wire-like feathers on its tail. It had a beautiful song, but it turned to a moan when it was captured.

Cactus Cat: This lynx-like cat is a native of the North American deserts. It sports a scythe-like protrusion on its front legs that it uses to cut off chunks of cactus on which it then dines.

Caiman: A crocodilian animal, the Caiman had human hands with fingers tipped with the talons of a bird of prey.

Cameleopardel: The ancient and medieval Europeans confused this creature with a giraffe. It was believed to be the offspring of a leopard and a camel, hence the name. It was said to be the size and height of a camel with the skin of a leopard and two long horns that curved backwards.

Carbuncle: In South American legend, this strange, little creature had a bright jewel growing on its forehead. The gem was reputed to have medicinal and magical powers.

Catoblepas: The Catoblepas, also known as the Gorgon, was described by Pliny the Elder in Roman times and Edward Topsell in the seventeenth century. It was a sluggish creature, somewhere between the size of a calf and a bull, and lived between Egypt and Ethiopia. It was covered with scales, and had hair only on its head, which was so heavy that it could not hold it up. It had small, useless wings, large, swine-like teeth and hands on the ends of its legs. Anyone who saw its eyes died instantly.

Ccoa: This Peruvian storm spirit took the form of a cat with a large head. Hail rained from its ears and eyes.

Cerastes: This two-horned, desert snake of Egypt, described by Pliny the Elder, buried itself in sand and moved its horns about to attract birds and small roadents to eat. It was reputed to be able to detect poisons and to ward off the evil eye.

Cerberus: In Greek and Roman mythology, this three-headed dog was the offspring of the monsters Typhon and Echidna. Cerberus guarded the gates of the Underworld, keeping the living out and the dead in. In Hercules' last labor, he captured Cerberus, but soon returned the dog to its rightful place.

Ch'i Lin: This Chinese unicorn had the body of a stag, the hooves of a horse, and a single, twelve foot long horn coming out from the middle of its forehead. It was multi-colored and impossible to capture. It sprang from the center of the earth and may have re-presented the earth. It only appeared when a great man was born.

Chimera: Another of the brood of Typhon and Echidna, the Chimera was an odd creature, having the front end of a lion, the middle part of a goat and a dragon's tail. It was said to have three heads as well: a goat's, a dragon's and a lion's. The hero Bellerophon, while riding the winged horse, Pegasus, killed the Chimera.

Chinese Celestial Dog: This supernatural creature had two sides. The light side helped drive off evil spirits. The dark side which was known to carry off children, was connected with comets and meteors.

Cinomolgus: This bird's name means "Cinnamon Bird" in Latin. It built its nest out of cinnamon sticks at the very top of tall trees so humans couldn't reach them. However, humans still knocked the sticks down by throwing rocks at the nest.

Cockatrice: This strange animal, also know as the Basilisk, was considered the King of Serpents. Described by Pliny the Elder, among others, it lived in the Sahara Desert in North Africa. Born of a round egg laid by a seven year old rooster, during the days of Sirius, the Dog Star, its egg was hatched by a toad or a snake on a dung heap. The Cockatrice had the head and feet of a cock and the wings, body and tail of a Wyvern, which was a small dragon. Its eyes were toad-like, and like those of the Catoblepas, had the ability to cause death. As if that were not enough, its breath was poisonous and it could only be killed by a weasel.

Cock of Dawn: This heavenly rooster of China lived in a tree in the Land of Sunrise at the far, eastern end of the world. He had gold feathers and three legs. All the roosters of the earth were allegedly hatched from eggs that he(!) laid.

Crocotta: This hyena-like beast, described like so many others by Pliny the Elder, was born of the mating of a wolf and a dog. The Crocotta had a rigid backbone and its jaw was a single tooth. It could imitate the voices of humans.

Feng: This bird was a three-legged Phoenix of China. It represented eternal love and lived in the heart of the sun.

Fire Drake: This was the typical dragon of European (particularly Norse and British) myth. It lived in caves and guarded hoards of gold. It was winged and of course, breathed fire.

Gargoyles: These ugly, stone creatures were developed from the drain pipes placed on cathedrals. They were believed to protect the cathedral from evil spirits. The word Gargoyle comes from "La Gourgille," which came from the word for throat, which is the same base from which the word gargle derived. Although most people associate Gargoyles with medieval churches, there are actually examples of of them dating back as far as the 5th Century B.C.

Gryphon: Although the gryphon, or griffin, was described by the Greek, Herodotus, the Roman, Pliny the Elder and the Englishman, Sir John Mandeville, it origins are even older, as its image is found in ancient Babylonia and Assyria. It was considerably larger than either an eagle or a lion, but it had the front end, including the feet and the wings of an eagle and the rear legs and the tail of a lion. Oddly, it had the pointed ears of an ass.

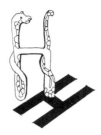

Hercinia: It was a jay sized bird whose eyes glowed in the dark like bright stars.

Hippocamp: This literal sea horse, although given its name by the Europeans, is found in the mythology of all countries. This creature was the steed of the sea god, Poseidon. It had the head and front legs of a horse, and the abdomen and tail of a fish. It had a fin instead of a mane and webbed feet. In addition to being found in classical mythology, it was well known in Celtic legend, as well as having been found in other cultures, from Romania to Iran to India.

Hippocerf: This strange creature of Medieval European legend was half stag and half horse. Its two sides pulled it in opposite directions, and thus it represented indecision.

Hippogryph: This creature, first described by the Italian poet, Aristo in his epic Orlando Furioso, combined the front part of a Gryphon with the rear of a horse. It lived in the moutains of the far northern part of the earth.

Hoop Snake: This snake was common to mythology the world over. It was suppose to move by inserting its tail in its mouth, thus forming a hoop, and rolling very quickly.

Hydra: Yet another of the numerous offspring of Typhon and Echidna, the Hydra was a nine-headed serpent. However, if one of its heads was cut off, two more grew in its place. It ravaged the swamps of Lerna, near Argos. In his second labor, Hercules killed the Hydra by cutting off each head and then used a torch to burn the neck so that no new heads could grow.

Ihuaivulu: This was a seven headed, Latin American, fire monster which lived near volcanos and was mountainous in size.

Kappa: A Japanese water spirit, the Kappa took the form of a monkey in a turtle shell with scaly, webbed limbs. On the top of its head was a bowl-shaped hollow which held water possessing magical powers. If treated with courtesy, it could be kind and had knowledge of the art of bone-setting. However, if one was not kind or was impolite, it would drown you. It liked to eat cucumbers and melons.

Kekeko: In Indonesian mythology, this talking bird was somewhat like a parrot. However, it could converse and give advice, rather than just mimicking the human voice. It was known to be especially kind to children.

Lacertus botrax: In Medieval legend, this creature was a variety of lizard with the head of a frog and human-like hands.

Lacertus saura: In Medieval lore, this was a variety of lizard that went blind in old age. It then went into a hole facing east and stretched towards the rising sun, which resulted in the return of its sight.

Leontophontes: There is no reliable description of this small creature, which was said to resemble plants. Its flesh was posionous to lions and because of this hunters used it as bait. Lions hated this creature and crushed it whenever they could.

Lesouik: One of many mythical shape shifters, this one came from Russia. It left no footprints behind it, no matter what kind of surface if walked upon.

Makara: The makara was the steed of the Indian moon god, Varuna. It was described in many ways, including one version in which it had the head of an elephant and the body of a fish. Being fairly large, it liked to spend its time in the ocean.

Mandrake: This strange plant had a root which looked exactly like a little man. It grew at the foot of a gallows tree. If it was picked, it screamed a scream which caused anyone who heard it to go mad and die. The most common method used to obtain it was to have a trained dog dig it up. Although the dog died, the plant supposedly had many magical powers, including bringing good luck to the owner. According to Pliny the Elder, the male Mandrakes were white, the female black.

Mermex: These ants were the size of mice. The soldiers were tusked, the workers not. They collected gold, as well as food and were mentioned in the mythology of many cultures, in slightly different variations.

Minotaur: In Greek mythology, the Minotaur was the monstrous offspring of the unnatural mating of Pasiphaë, the wife of King Minos of Crete, and a bull. The Minotaur had the head of a bull and the body of a man. King Minos had the architect Daedalus design a labyrinth in which to keep his stepson, the Minotaur. In order to feed him, Minos received a tribute of seven Athenian youths and seven Athenian maidens every nine years. This was finally ended when Theseus, the son of King Aegeus of Athens, went to Crete as part of a tribute to the Minotaur. He used a ball of yarn, given to him by Minos' daughter, Ariadne, as a guide so as not to get lost in the maze. He killed the Minotaur, either with his bare hands or possibly with a sword given him by Ariadne.

Mixcoatl: The Aztec god of the chase, Mixcoatl was a cloud serpent or dragon, with rabbit or deer features.

Morou-Ngou: An African, leopard-like creature, a denizen of the water, it had webbed paws and was considered one of the fastest animals in both the water and on the land.

Nemean Lion: Another offspring of Typhon and Echidna, the Nemean Lion was enormous, with impenetrable skin. It plagued the region of Nemea in Peloponnesus. It was finally killed by Hercules, who strangled it to death and ever after wore its skin.

Nuddu-Waighai: This possum-like animal, adorned with wings, is an Australian Aboriginal myth, which reputedly hated hunters.

Nyah-Gwaheh: This huge, bear-like animal was attributed with magical powers by the Iroquois tribe of North America, and was considered to be a bear spirit.

On-Niont: A Huron Indian myth, this mountain-like serpent was so big that it could pierce mountains, but was never seen.

Oshadagea: This dew eagle of the Iroquois Indians of North America carried a lake in the hollow of its back. It flew over the earth and sprinkled the world with dew.

Palraujuk: This was an unusual dragon, in that instead of breathing fire, it blew ice and cold air from its mouth.

Panther (Cherokee): In Cherokee Legend, the Panther, or Mountain Lion, was sacred, and had night vision.

Panther (European): In European Legend, the Panther looked like a real-life leopard. However, this creature had extremely sweet breath and a beautiful voice, which it may have used to lure small animals to their deaths. It was more generally thought all animals, except the Dragon, loved and admired the Panther.

Panther (Polynesian): The sacred Panther of Polynesia had flames emerging from its head, back and legs.

Parandrus: The Europeans believed this animal lived in Ethiopia and had the body of a bear and the head and legs of a Stag or an Ibex. It had the ability to change its color to match that of objects near it.

Persian Simurgh: This creature may have been a bird with the head, teeth and paws of a dog, or a dog with the body, wings and feathers of a bird. It was a beneficial creature, living in the land where the Soma Tree grows, being guarded by 99,999 attendants and a fish. Later legends described the Simurgh as an enormous bird living in the Alburz Mountains of Persia, whose feathers had medicinal uses.

Peryton: This composite bird and deer had the body of the deer and the wings and feathers of a bird. Perytons used to congregate over the area where Atlantis sank. The strangest feature of this vicious animal was that it cast the shadow of a man. Some believed that it was the spirit of a man who died far from his homeland and that the Peryton had to kill a man in order to regain its true form and then be able to rest.

Phoenix: This large bird symbolized eternal life. Supposedly it lived in the Arabian desert for around five hundred years. It then built a large nest at the top of a tall tree, which was set aflame by the sun. The Phoenix died, but from its ashes sprang a new Phoenix. Once the new Phoenix was strong enough, it carried the ashes of its father to the Temple of the Sun in the Egyptian city of Heliopolis.

Ping Feng: This black pig of China had a head on each end of its body. It was said to live in the Land of Magic Waters.

Pooka: In Irish legend, the Pooka was a mischievous being who often appeared in the form of a horse or a donkey, but could take any form. Some said it was malevolent and wore chains which it shook in order to frighten travellers. Others said it was friendly to those who did it a favor and could even grant the ability to understand the language of animals.

Poua-kai: In the legends of the Maori peoples, who are native to New Zealand, this large, eagle-like bird preyed on humans. Despite the fact that it constantly watched the Maoris from its eyrie, it was eventually killed by a band of warriors.

Puk: In Baltic myth, this small, four-footed dragon brought

treasure to a household. (The Baltic peoples live in Northeastern Europe, on the shores of the Baltic Sea, primarily in Lithuania and Latvia.)

Qata: Arabian in origin, the Qata was reputed to be the fastest animal on earth. It was ram-like, with reversed horns..

Remora: This small fish was found in European legend. It travelled in large schools and attached itself to the bottoms of ships, which impeded the boat's progress enormously. Strangely enough, this fish also had feet and it was rumored that it could be used as a love charm.

Roc: An enormous Arabian bird, the Roc may have been a relative of the Persian Simurgh. Rocs were featured in many of the stories of the *Arabian Nights*, particularly those featuring Sinbad the Sailor. Rocs were believed to be so large they could pick up elephants in their talons. They were identified with the Rook in chess.

Rompo: Found in both African and Indian legends, the Rompo was a bizarre combination of several different animals. It had a hare's head, a man's ears, a long body and tail, the front feet of a badger and the back feet of a bear. Little is known of it other than that it was a scavenger.

Salamander: A small lizard, described by Pliny the Elder, the Salamander was believed to breath fire, and to have the ability to put out a fire by walking through it. It was also, supposedly, one of the most venomous creatures on earth. It was frequently considered to be the personification of the element fire.

Sea Dog: The Sea Dog was a heraldic creature that appeared to be of the Talbot variety of dog, except that it had scales, webbed feet and a beaver's tail. It was a natural enemy of the Sea Hare.

Sea Lion: This was a heraldic animal which had the upper body of a lion and the lower body of a fish.

Sea Serpent: A mythical, giant snake or legless dragon, of huge size, the Sea Serpent was found in mythology all over the world.

Skinfaxi: In Norse mythology, this horse was the steed of day. He had a golden mane, from which golden light spread in streaks across the sky.

Tazelwurm: There were several versions of the Tazelwurm. One said it was a small, shy, winged lizard that lived in isolation in the Swiss mountain caves. Another said it was gigantic, fire-breathing, fierce serpent of Germanic origin, living in the caves of the mountains of Austria, Bavaria and Switzerland.

Tree Goose: According to Medieval scholars, these geese grew on certain trees in Ireland. They remained attached to the tree until they were fully grown, at which point they fell off into a body of water, and then flew or swam away.

Unicorn: In the original legends of Medieval Europe, the Unicorn was a small animal somewhat like a goat, which had only one horn in the middle of its head. The idea of the Unicorn as a horse-like creature only appeared later. It was believed that the Unicorn could only be caught by using a virgin as bait. On seeing her, it would find its way into her lap, and then could be easily caught. The horn of the Unicorn was thought to have magical powers when ground into powder, much like the horn of the Rhinoceros, with which it was often confused, even by Pliny the Elder.

Vampire: Vampires were a myth of Slavic origin. An evil spirit inhabited the body of an unblessed person, reanimating the body at night, at which time it turned into a bat. The

bat flew through open windows and sucked the blood of sleeping individuals who then became vampires as well.

Volkh: This shape-shifting creature, also of Slavic origin, was the guardian of the city of Kiev, the medieval capital of Russia. It could appear as an animal, a bird, or an insect and had many other magical powers, including that of protecting people with whom it came in contact.

Werewolf: Although "were-animals" were a myth native to most of the world, the European myth of the Werewolf is most commonly known. A Werewolf was usually a person who transformed into a wolf at night. It was sometimes possible to end the spell that caused the transformation by pointing out and identifying the "wolf" while in its human form.

Wyvern: The European legend of the Wyvern claimed it was a small variety of Dragon, with two legs and bat-like wings. The word Wyvern derives from the French word "wivere," which means both viper and life. In Heraldry, it represented both war and pestilence.

Yale: In Medieval myth, the Yale was a spotted or black antelope-like creature, with the snout of a boar and the tail of an elephant. Its horns were unique for they branched in opposite directions, and could swivel 360 degrees. It was a Heraldic symbol.

Yata Garusu: This Japanese, three legged crow was a messenger for the sun goddess, Ameratsu and was believed to cause sun spots.

(NOTE: There are many variations of most myths, even within a single culture. Similar myths and mythic themes are found in far flung countries. As well as verbal variations in myth, there are many visual varieties of the "same" mythical beast.)